Bertrand Arthur Henry Wilberforce, Henry Edward Manning

Dominican missions and martyrs in Japan

Bertrand Arthur Henry Wilberforce, Henry Edward Manning

Dominican missions and martyrs in Japan

ISBN/EAN: 9783741191633

Manufactured in Europe, USA, Canada, Australia, Japa

Cover: Foto ©Andreas Hilbeck / pixelio.de

Manufactured and distributed by brebook publishing software
(www.brebook.com)

Bertrand Arthur Henry Wilberforce, Henry Edward Manning

Dominican missions and martyrs in Japan

PREFACE

AMONG the many and wonderful creations of the Catholic Church, the Order of Friars Preachers has a character peculiar to itself. The Orders of S. Benedict and of S. Francis have thrown out many various off-shoots from the old stem: the Order of S. Dominic has continued always compact and self-contained. For six hundred years it has retained its unity. This fidelity to its original type is not, however, from a lifeless sterility, but from the singular precision in its discipline and its traditions. It has been eminent both in the Schools and in the Missions of the Church. It has a multitude of saints, of doctors and of martyrs. In one only century, we are told in this book, that is from 1234 to 1334, 13,370 of its members received the crown of martyrdom. The following pages are intended to record its missions in Japan alone. No country of modern times, except Corea, has so cruelly shed the blood of those who brought to it the tidings of peace. In 1640, when the Portuguese ambassadors were massacred at Nagasaki, their remains were sent back to Macao with this inscription : " As long as the sun continues to shine on the earth, let no Christian dare to enter Japan, and let every one understand that if the King of Spain himself, or the God of the Christians, or even the great Zaca (one of the principal deities of Japan) should violate this law, they shall be punished with death." * Japan has kept its word. Persecution has never relented whensoever Christians have been found. These cruelties have been instigated sometimes by the English, sometimes by the Dutch. It is curious to read the same accusations of treason against the supremacy of the civil power and of harbouring priests in Japan as our own history records. Of the tortures endured by these true Apostles of Jesus Christ it is hard to form any adequate conception. In the Great

* Page 157.

Martyrdom, five-and-twenty were burnt at the stake, and thirty-three were beheaded. At another time we read of those who were for sixteen hours burning in the fire, or three days lingering on the cross; of children of four and of three years of age, of infants carried to martyrdom in their mothers' arms. These glorious annals read like a description of the first Christians in the Gardens of Nero. There is something touching and beautiful to find mingled with the priests and apostles of the Church the poor native men and women, members of the Confraternity of the Holy Rosary, who went to martyrdom, their beads in their hands, with the invocation, "Queen of the Holy Rosary, pray for us." So deeply had the faith penetrated among the people that 37,000 natives rose in arms in 1638 to defend their religion. Though overwhelmed and cut down, the faith lived on in secret; and in our day thousands have been found who, without pastors or sacraments, have handed on their belief inviolate, with its three sure tests—

the authority of Rome, the celibacy of the Priesthood, the loving veneration of the Mother of God. This beautiful little book gives a noble picture of the supernatural power, unity, and authority of the Church. In these sharp conflicts are to be seen side by side the sons of S. Augustine, of S. Francis, S. Dominic, and S. Ignatius, labouring together and mingling their blood in one stream for the love of the Good Shepherd who laid down His life for the sheep. Truly Japan is the mother of martyrs, and Father Francis Morales spoke with the spirit of his crucified Lord when, thirsting for martyrdom, he cried out, "O my brethren, how beautiful is the land of Japan!" May God pour out upon us here in England the same spirit of love and of sacrifice, of missionary zeal, fortitude and self-oblation, for the sake of England and of the nations without God in the world.

✠ HENRY EDWARD,
Archbishop of Westminster.

Feast of S. Mark, 1869.

CONTENTS

The sources from which I have almost entirely drawn this narrative are the three following works :

1.—*Historia de la Provincia del S. Rosario de Filipinas, Japon y China.* Por el Illust. Señor Don Fray Diego Advarte. 1693.

2.—*I Martiri dell' Ordine dè Predicatori chi, uccisi per la Fede nel Giappone, furono Ascritti al Catalogo de Beati dal Regnante Sommo Pontefice Pio IX.* Compilato sopra Autentici Documenti dal P. Fr. Pio Tommaso Masetti. Roma, 1868.

3.—*Missions Dominicaines dans l'extrême Orient.* Par le R. P. Fr. André Marie. Paris, 1865.

I state this to avoid the necessity of giving my authority at the foot of every page.

B. W.

DOMINICAN MISSIONARIES

IN JAPAN.

———✠———

CHAPTER I.

Introduction of Christianity into Japan. Rise of Persecution. The First Martyrs.

HE Order of Friars-Preachers, founded by the great patriarch, S. Dominic, is essentially a missionary Order. Its spirit is at once monastic and apostolic, forming a link between the ancient contemplative Orders and the modern active Congregations. The object of S. Dominic in his foundation was to form an Order of teachers and preachers who, living under a rule obliging them to all the distinctive observances of monastic life, might impart to the Church the fruits of their contemplation.

In the early part of the fourteenth century
Benedict XII., a Cistercian monk, filled the Chair
of S. Peter.   Certain members of his Order petitioned the Pontiff to change the constitutions of
the Friars-Preachers, representing that the severity
of their rule unfitted them for the laborious
duties of the apostolic life.   The General Chapter
of the Order, then assembled in Valentia, considered what answer to these complaints would
most influence the mind of the Pope and save
the Order from the threatened disaster.   It was
proposed to compute the number of martyrs the
friars had given to the Church during one century, from 1234 to 1334.   The number amounted
to 13,370.   This argument was conclusive, and
the rule remained inviolate.

S. Dominic himself was unable, as he ardently
desired, to preach to the heathen and to shed
his blood for the faith, but in the persons of
his children he has evangelized the world ; in
every nation his apostolic voice has gone forth,
in every land his white scapular has been dyed
with the blood of martyrdom.   By establishing
the " Order of Truth " he has carried the light
of faith to nations sitting in darkness and in
the shadow of death.

The heroic men who formed the Province of
the Rosary in the Philippine Islands, had drunk
deeply of the true spirit of their Order, and from
their number were chosen the missionaries who

shed their blood in Japan, and whose labours and sufferings are briefly recorded in these pages. Their lives supply a sufficient answer to complaints such as those addressed to Benedict XII. by the Cistercians. They united perfectly the monastic and the apostolic spirit. The grace to perform the one was drawn from a rigid observance of the other. One isolated missionary, overwhelmed with active duties, besides the austerities of his rule, divided his day chorally, and recited his office as though he were in community. When two were together, they recited the midnight office, and observed the rule of conventual life. The conversion of thousands who became saints and martyrs was the consequence.

A "History of the Japanese Missions" has already appeared in English, but no information is given of the share taken in the work by the Dominican Fathers. This is surprising when we consider the universal spread of the Rosary Confraternity throughout the Christian part of the empire, and the prominent position of the friars from A.D. 1601 till the destruction of the missions. Pius IX. chose the feast of S. Catherine of Siena for granting permission to proceed to the Beatification of July, 1867, because "so many women of invincible courage among the Japanese martyrs had followed her in the paths of virtue" by being Tertiaries of S. Dominic. It is to be regretted that the gifted authoress of the "History of the Missions of Japan " was not aware of these facts.

In many points of view the Japanese are an extraordinary people. They had reached a high degree of civilization centuries before the Romans set foot in Britain, and if they had been converted to Christianity at an early date, they might have escaped that state of decay they fell into for centuries, the result of the corruptions of idolatry, and the apathy produced by isolation from their fellow-men. The ecclesiastical history of the Japanese brings out their good and bad qualities in strong relief. The natural virtues of the people attracted them to the Church, and those virtues, elevated by grace, presented the finest examples of genuine Christian character. The dread of foreign influence induced the government to extirpate the Faith by fire and sword.

The collection of islands which, grouped under one government, form the empire of Japan, lie east of the mainland of Asia, and were discovered by the Portuguese in the fifteenth century. The government until the recent changes was despotic, and the line of the emperors, or Mikados as they were called, is extremely ancient, reaching back to at least five hundred years before the Christian era. But at the end of the twelfth century, or nearly A.D. 1300, changes were introduced which are thus described by Father L. C. Casartelli, in an article of great interest in the Dublin Review, entitled " The Catholic Church in Japan." *

" Yoritano, the all-powerful minister of the Mikado, established the curious system of government known as the Shogunate, which endured till so recent a date as 1868. This system resembles nothing so much as that of the ' mayors of the palace ' under the later Merovingian kings. The Shogun (the name was long known in Europe under the quasi-Chinese name of " Tycoon ") was commander-in-chief of the forces, and also vice-regent of the empire. And though for long periods he was actually the *de facto* ruler, still during the whole eight centuries of the Shogunate, this potentate always scrupulously observed the outward show of reverence for and absolute dependance upon the emperor, whose humble servant he professed to be, and whose commission he always received for the performance of his duties."

The town most interesting to Catholics, in consequence of its being formerly the headquarters of Christianity, is that of Nagasaki. This town is the capital of the island of Kiou-Siou, and, though by no means the most populous, it is one of the most important cities of the empire, as being the only port at which, for nearly two hundred years, any foreign commerce was tolerated. High mountains shut in the town on the land

* *Dublin Review* for April, 1895.

side, but the coast slopes off gently towards the
sea, forming an advantageous position for a harbour, which is generally much frequented by
native as well as Chinese and European vessels.
Nagasaki, as the reader will presently see, has
justly received the name of the Holy City, the
City of the Martyrs.

Very soon after the discovery of the empire
by the Portuguese, missionaries sailed from Goa
for the various islands of eastern Asia, and in
1530, we are told, a Dominican father endeavoured to reach Japan, but was killed on
the way by the inhabitants of the island of
Loo-Choo.

Almighty God had reserved the work of sowing
the first seeds of gospel truth in Japan to the great
apostle of the Society of Jesus, S. Francis
Xavier. The career of this marvellous man, the
faithful imitator of the first apostles, the glory and
wonder of the Church in the sixteenth century, is
too well known to need more than a passing mention. But it was impossible to pass over in silence
the work of one who, Pius IX. has declared, merits
to be called the apostle of Japan, while at the
same time to enter into the details of his life
would lead us from our immediate subject. It will
be sufficient, then, to remind the reader that
S. Francis was one of the first companions and
one of the greatest children whom God gave
to His servant the illustrious S. Ignatius. Chosen

by God for the sublime work of the foreign missions, S. Francis was despatched to India, where the life he led, his preaching, his example, and the marvels God worked by his means, have made his name glorious in the whole Church. While at Goa the saint, meeting a Japanese noble who was overwhelmed with troubles which had driven him from his native land, converted him to Christianity. Once in the Church himself, he begged S. Francis to go to Japan, and confer the same happiness on his poor fellow-countrymen. Much persuasion was not necessary to induce S. Francis to undertake any enterprise, however dangerous or hopeless it might appear, if only it would tend to God's glory and the good of souls. He preached therefore for two years in Japan, and that short space was enough to convert incredible numbers to the true faith. After thus planting the Cross in the empire he left the work in the hands of others of the Society, while he departed to evangelize the immense pagan empire of China. But God accepted the will for the deed, and took His faithful servant to an eternal reward within sight of the Chinese coast on the 2nd of December, 1552.

Meanwhile the other Jesuit fathers were imitating his example and converting thousands of the Japanese. In many provinces they founded permanent missions, building churches and colleges, and establishing schools for the instruction of the natives. For a considerable period they were left unmolested by the government, but under Taiko-Sama this favourable state of affairs altered.

" Taiko-Sama (literally ' Lord Taiko ') was in reality the Prime Minister, Commander-in-Chief, and Vice-regent, known in Japanese history as Hideyoshi. He was not emperor, and never obtained even the exalted title of Shogan, but was content with the lower one of Kwambahu, though his power was none the less absolute." *

The persecution which he began has been attributed to different causes, the hatred the bonzes entertained towards Christianity, the natural jealousy in so exclusive a people of a foreign religion, all no doubt encouraged and increased by the devil. " But whatever dislike to Christianity had been growing up in his mind was fanned into a flame by the firmness and constancy of certain Christian maidens who refused to yield to his lustful passions and preferred death to sin."

The first edict was published in 1587, banishing all foreign religious teachers from Japan under pain of death. Nagasaki was the only exception, for, as many Europeans resided there, priests were allowed to remain for their sake, though forbidden to leave the town. Still they managed secretly to continue their apostolic journeys into the different provinces of the

* F. Casartelli, *Dublin Review.*

empire, and baptised sixty-five thousand adults, besides multitudes of children. In the year 1593 they were joined by some fathers of the Seraphic Order of S. Francis of Assisi, who immediately began to evangelize the people and to reap an abundant harvest of souls.

Shortly afterwards, however, an unfortunate event took place, which excited the anger of Taiko-Sama against the Spaniards and Portuguese, and resulted in the outbreak of a persecution which never really ended till every missionary had been either put to death or driven from the country. A Spanish vessel, laden with valuable merchandise from the Philippine Islands, was thrown by a tempest on the coast of Japan, and the crew being saved, certain persons represented to the emperor that this was only the first step of a preconcerted plan, by which it was intended to subject the whole empire to the Spanish yoke. Taiko-Sama believed these reports, and in consequence issued edicts commanding the immediate massacre of all the Christians in every part of the empire. This command was not fully carried out. The princes ruling over the various provinces of the empire frequently assumed a great deal of independence in their own government, and in this instance they modified the cruel command of their feudal lord. The governor of Macao also petitioned that the punishment might be confined to those strangers who had entered Japan from the Philippine Islands, and whom the emperor had been informed were emissaries of the Spanish government. According to this modified edict of persecution, the fathers of the Society of Jesus who had come from Macao were released on condition of immediately withdrawing from the country, but the Franciscan missionaries were thrown into prison and sentenced to be crucified.

The governor of Nagasaki had imprisoned three Japanese who had entered the Society of Jesus, and these also, together with seventeen natives, members of the Third Order of S. Francis, were included in the same sentence. Twenty-six crosses were planted on a hill near the city of Nagasaki on the 5th of February, 1597, and the martyrs bravely suffered to the last, without one of them failing in the trial. They were the proto-martyrs of Japan, the first of a long catalogue of heroic Christians who sacrificed their lives for Christ. Their names were first enrolled in the list of the beatified by Urban VIII. in 1629, and in our own day they were solemnly canonized by Pope Pius IX., on the 8th of June, 1862, in the presence of a vast concourse of bishops from every part of the world.*

* For details of the outbreak of this first persecution, and the arrival, labours, and heroic martyrdom of the Franciscan Missionaries, see the pamphlet of the Rev. Father Emmanuel Kenners, O.S.F., "A Brief Sketch of the Lives

CHAPTER II.

Entrance of the Dominicans into Japan.

AR from daunting the courage of the missionaries, this outbreak of persecution only seemed to stimulate them to new exertions ; and as in every age and every country God appears to demand the blood of martyrs as the price of the gift of faith, so in Japan we find that multitudes were gathered into the fold of the Church immediately after the sacrifice of the first martyrs. In the year 1599 alone the concealed missionaries of the Society of Jesus baptized more than seventy thousand natives ; so that unless a persecution of almost unparalleled barbarity had arisen, the whole empire would very shortly have been Christian. It had long been felt that the labourers were indeed few to gather in a harvest so abundant, and more than ten years before the Jesuit missionaries had joined with many of the native Christians in an earnest petition to the Friars-Preachers of the Philippine Islands to send assistance to the Japanese mission.

and Martyrdom of the Franciscan Saints canonized by Pope Pius the Ninth."

It was not from any lack of zeal in the work that this pressing invitation was not accepted. The Province of the Holy Rosary —established in the Spanish colony of the Philippine Islands—had, from its very foundation, been remarkable for the apostolic labours of its members. Dominic of Salazer, the first Bishop of Manilla, may be considered as its principal founder, for it was at his earnest desire that Father John Chrysostom repaired to Europe from America, to seek for subjects to form a province in the newly-discovered islands. Having obtained letters of authorization from Paul Constable of Ferrara, the Master-General of the Order —who also made him Vicar-General of the Congregation of the Holy Rosary in the Philippine Islands,—Father John Chrysostom found little difficulty in meeting with companions ready to undertake a work so conducive to the salvation of souls; and having at last made a satisfactory arrangement with the Spanish government he started from Europe with thirty-two friars of the Order. On the voyage, in spite of the hardships they were obliged to endure, these fervent religious observed their rule to the letter. They assembled at regular hours for the Office—which they recited together—and for the common meditations; they kept the fasts and abstinences prescribed by the rule, without taking any advantage of their privileges as travellers, and they took their meals in silence, listening to a reader, as if they were still in their convent refectory. Often during the voyage they preached to the sailors of the vessel, and had the comfort of leading many of them to a better life. It was the custom to pass through Mexico in order to reach the Philippines, so that there were two long and perilous voyages before arriving at their destination. Some were left in America, others sent to Macao, while three died on the voyage, so that only fifteen reached Manilla, where they were welcomed with the utmost joy by Dominic of Salazer. This was on the eve of S. Mary Magdalen's day, in the year 1587, which may be considered as the date of the foundation of the Province of the Holy Rosary.

No time was lost by these apostolic men after their arrival. They at once began their labours among the natives and also sent missionaries to Formosa and other islands. The reason that obliged them to refuse the request of those who invited them into Japan, was the difficulty caused by a Bull of Pope Gregory XIII. by which the missions of Japan were given exclusively to the Fathers of the Society of Jesus. The Holy Father thought it wise to insure unity of government and design in these difficult missions, and this would be effected by admitting only one Order into the empire. This decree had been abrogated in favour of the Order of S. Francis by Sixtus V., and therefore, after the persecution had so sadly diminished the number of apostolic labourers, it was decided that the Dominicans also might lawfully enter Japan. The Jesuit Fathers, like S. Peter and S. John, found that they were unable to haul in the full draught of fish that God had given them, and so, like the Apostles, they turned to their brethren for help.

The Dominicans of Manilla rejoiced exceedingly when the difficulties raised by the Pope's Bull were surmounted, and the Bishop of Manilla favoured the project of sending fathers to Japan. But it was some little time before all their hopes were realized. Their desire was increased by the arrival in Manilla of some Japanese vessels, in which many of the sailors were Christians. These men were delighted with the churches of Manilla, which they constantly visited with great devotion, and amongst others that of the Friars-Preachers, which was one of the largest and finest in the city.

Father Francis de Morales, whom God destined to shed his blood for the faith, was then prior of the convent, and used often to converse with the Japanese about their native country, its government, its people, and the prospects of Christianity. They represented the people, and many even in influential positions, as very favourable to the true faith, and begged the friars to send priests to carry them the light of Christ's

Gospel. One of these Japanese, John Sandaya, particularly struck Father Francis de Morales by the fervour of his piety, and this man pleaded most earnestly with the good prior for the salvation of his fellow-countrymen. His ship was from the kingdom of Satsuma, and the captain undertook with the utmost joy to take the missionaries on board. It was considered more prudent, however, to discover what view the King of Satsuma would take of this proceeding, and therefore a letter was sent, in John Sandaya's ship, from the provincial to the King of Satsuma, asking permission to land in his kingdom. The answer was most favourable. The king sent a ship to convey them to Cogiqui, a port of his kingdom, and also a very gracious letter by the hand of Leo Fuisayemon, a native Christian, promising a cordial reception to the Fathers. He asked for twenty, but the resources of the province could not supply so many, and Father Francis de Morales, the Prior of Manilla, was sent with only four companions. All were desirous to be of the number, but those who had the happiness were Fathers Thomas Fernandez, Alphonsus de Mena, Thomas of the Holy Ghost, surnamed Zumarraga, and Brother John of Abadia. This devoted little band, after tenderly embracing their brethren, set sail on the feast of the Holy Trinity, a fitting day for an enterprise so greatly for God's honour. They were in extreme poverty, having nothing but what was given them by a few devout people as alms. During the voyage they were detained some time by calms, but after promising some Masses of thanksgiving, a favourable breeze sprang up, which soon wafted them into the harbour of Cogiqui.

On landing they were lodged in a heathen temple, which was done, says the old Spanish author, by the providence of God, in order that the light of Faith might shine first from that very spot which the devil had especially usurped for his own worship. The priest of the temple, seeing that the sight of the idols troubled the missionaries, took them to a part of the temple that was unoccupied, and here the Fathers erected an altar, having first blessed the place and cleansed it from all heathenish defilement. Over this altar—the first Dominican altar in Japan—they placed an image of our Lord, which had been given them by a Spanish gentleman of Manilla. The people flocked around them in crowds, listening to their words with great attention, and manifesting the utmost respect for their persons, especially for Father Francis de Morales, by whose appearance they were fascinated. Naturally curious, they noticed everything about these new preachers, their persons, speech, habits, actions, and penitential exercises, and especially the modest demeanour they displayed in all their actions. They admired, also, the harmony and brotherly love in which the friars lived, and the happy mixture of joy and gravity which appeared on their countenances.

Before long the Fathers were visited by a large cavalcade of the nobles of the kingdom, sent by the king to lead the religious with great state into the royal presence. After a great deal of ceremony the Japanese offered the friars horses and a large retinue, that they might proceed with fitting dignity to the capital city. No argument, however, could prevail upon the fathers to mount on horseback; they declared that it would be contrary to their constitutions and the custom of their province, and that their laws must be observed. They journeyed therefore on foot, and were received with great rejoicing by the king and his court, being lodged in one of the best houses of the city. In return for the royal favours the friars presented some glasses to the king, which he valued highly. At a feast in the royal palace to which the missionaries were invited, some of the courtiers objecting to the austerity of their manner of life, they defended themselves to the king's satisfaction. After this they found it necessary to decline with great civility any further feasting, saying that they had come into Japan to preach the faith to the people.

The success that attended their first entrance into Japan did not continue long unchecked. The

C

bonzes very naturally grew jealous of the high
honours paid to these strangers by the king, and
of the veneration shown them by the people.
They endeavoured therefore to frighten the king,
and to prevent him from giving his consent to
the erection of a church and priory as the
fathers desired.   The same argument was used
which we hear every day urged against the
Church in Europe. Worldly prosperity, said the
bonzes, has never yet attended those Japanese
who have embraced this new doctrine ; they have
become a prey to their enemies, have fallen under
the displeasure of the emperor, and have been
ruined by following this strange religion. The
kingdom of Satsuma, they urged, owes its prosperity and the victories it has gained over its
enemies to the powerful protection of Faquimore,
the god of war ; and woe betide you, O king, if
you desert the god of your fathers !

These representations so frightened the king,
who was naturally weak-minded and timorous,
that the missionaries were unable to obtain his
consent to their building a church and priory,
or to preach and baptize openly among the
people. For a long time they lived together in
one apartment in the house of a heathen, who
was firmly rooted in his idolatrous practices and
much prejudiced against Christianity. This man
closely watched the manner of life followed by
the fathers, and was forced to admire the extreme

patience, regularity, penance, and love of prayer, which he saw them practising, and, above all, the contempt they manifested for the goods and comforts of the world. The one apartment they inhabited was used for their church, in which the Office and Masses were said, and afterwards for refectory, kitchen and dormitory. Their good example did more than excite mere admiration in the mind of their host, for before long he asked for instruction in the faith, received baptism, and persevered in many good works till death.

The greatest treasure which the fathers had in their little oratory was a beautiful image of our Lady of the Holy Rosary, which was much admired by the Japanese, and which the missionaries carried to the court, that they might thus have an opportunity of explaining the chief mysteries of faith. In spite of the admiration which the king could not help feeling for the doctrines and persons of the friars, the fear of the emperor's displeasure at last fairly overcame him, and he consented to the petition of the bonzes that they should be banished to a small island called Quogiqui, which was only thinly inhabited by a few poor fishermen. Here the missionaries suffered very much from cold and hunger, but they rejoiced that thus they were able to follow strictly the example of their holy founder, S. Dominic, in his love and practice of poverty. They depended for the small pittance of

rice and fish, which was their food, on the kind-
ness of the heathen fishermen. Sometimes they
could obtain nothing, and once when in great
distress they were relieved by a poor native who
took compassion on them, and for his reward
received the gift of faith.   During this time of
trial, they were animated by a holy spirit of
emulation for strict observance, not willing to be
outdone by their brethren of the Philippine
Islands, and after a time this faithfulness had
its reward. The friendship of the king was again
won when he saw the patience they displayed
in suffering, and their indifference to the things
of this world, and in the year 1606 he granted
them the long-desired permission to build a
church and house in the city of Quiodomari.
They dedicated this first church of the Order
in Japan in honour of our Lady of the Holy
Rosary, whom in all their troubles they had ever
found to be a tender and loving Mother. The
first Mass was celebrated in this new church
on the feast of the Visitation of the Blessed
Virgin.

From this settlement the friars were able
to make apostolic journeys, administering the
sacraments to the Christians in their houses, and
baptizing the heathens they converted. In the
town of Yenquchi particularly, there was a noble
Japanese lady, a widow, living with her young
son whom she was bringing up a Christian. At

her house the friars were constant and welcome visitors, saying Mass for the family, and instructing them fully in the duties of their religion. This good lady falling ill, Father Thomas of the Holy Ghost and Father Alphonsus de Mena were immediately sent for, from whom she received the last sacraments. Afterwards when lying at the point of death, her only anxiety was lest after her departure her youthful son might be perverted from the Christian faith, and she therefore exacted from the guardians of his estate a promise that he should be educated in the faith, and also earnestly exhorted him to remain a steadfast Christian. The young man never forgot this promise made to his dying mother, and afterwards during the persecution he gave up his estate by the advice of the fathers, lest he might be tempted to abandon his religion. This is mentioned as an example of the fervour of these new Christians.

Hitherto the friars had confined their apostolic labours to the single kingdom of Satsuma, but after fully establishing their church and house at Quiodomari, it was considered time to endeavour to form missions in other parts of the empire. Wherever they went, Christians were found who had not been able to receive the holy sacraments for many years, sometimes not having seen a priest since their baptism. The kingdom of Figen or Fixen, which was the richest

and most thickly populated in the empire, particularly attracted the apostolic zeal of the friars, and
accordingly Father Francis Morales sent Father
Alphonsus de Mena to see if an entrance could
be obtained into that province. Father Alphonsus
started on this journey like the disciples our
Lord sent forth, without provision for the way,
fortified only by the blessing of his superior and
the prayers of his brethren. God's providence
did not forsake him. On his journey he met
the captain of a Japanese vessel, whom he
discovered to be a fervent Christian, and this
good man was of the utmost assistance in obtaining permission from the King of Figen to build
churches in his province. The question was
referred by the king to a learned bonze, called
Gaco, whose wisdom was held in the highest
estimation by the emperor and all Japan. Father
Alphonsus at first feared that this must settle
the matter against him, but God moved this man
to advise the king to give the desired permission.
Father Alphonsus, therefore, was enabled by the
king's favour to build three churches with houses
attached ; the principal one being at a place
called Famamachi, which was placed under the
patronage of our Lady of the Rosary. These
churches were, of course, poor in the extreme,
and the houses still poorer, but they acted as
centres from which missionary journeys could
be made, and rendered it possible to celebrate

Mass with greater reverence, and to follow the observances of the Order.

The fickle King of Satsuma, who had invited the friars into his province, and, as we have seen, for a time greatly favoured them, terrified lest the emperor might become hostile to him, and excited by the representations of the bonzes, sent them peremptory orders, in 1609, to leave his kingdom entirely. Father Francis Morales found that it was hopeless to endeavour to change the king's purpose, and so, with a heavy heart at the deserted condition of his converts, he departed for other provinces. He sent a Father into the imperial city of Tokyo, where the emperor resided, and, by the blessing of God, a church was built, in which the first Mass was said on the conversion of St. Paul, 1610. Another mission was also established in the city of Osaca.* Father Francis Morales himself went to Nagasaki, the capital of Christianity in Japan, taking with him some lepers, for whom he had founded a hospital, his charity not allowing him to leave these poor sufferers to the mercy of the heathen. Here he shortly afterwards founded a church, under the invocation of our Lady of the Rosary and

---

* Osaca is a large seaport town on the south-east coast of Hondo Island, 250 miles south of Kyoto, to which there is now a railway. It is the principal commercial centre of Japan, exports tea, silk and other goods, and has a population of over 350,000.

S. Dominic, which remained until the destruction of the Church in Japan.

Between 1607 and 1612 six more Fathers of the Order arrived from Manilla, accompanied by a lay-brother. Their names were — Fathers John of the Angels, John of S. Thomas, Hyacinth Orphanel, Alphonsus Naverette, Dominic de Valderama, and Balthazar Fort. Their manner of life is described in a letter addressed to Father Diego Advarte, in 1608, by Fathers Alphonsus de Mena and Thomas of the Holy Ghost. It is translated from Father Meynard's work :

" You know the penitential manner of life led by our fathers of the Province of the Holy Rosary as to food and clothing, and also as to the choir offices, preaching, and the constant apostolic journeys they are obliged to make, in order to visit and to encourage the scattered Christians. We follow the same observance, and although there are only two religious in each province of Japan, we rise exactly at midnight, to recite Matins and make our meditation."

At this time, during the short period of comparative tranquillity before the outbreak of the tremendous storm of persecution shortly to follow, the kingdom of Figen was one of the most successful fields of missionary labour. After the entrance of the Dominican fathers described above, the Christians enjoyed perfect peace, and the missionaries were allowed free action in the

exercise of their zeal.   Father Alphonsus de
Mena, with Fathers John of the Angels and
Hyacinth Orphanel, were indefatigable in their
work of charity; the more so as events that
frequently happened warned them that their
opportunity would probably be short, and that
the time of trial was approaching.   Thus the
Jesuit missionaries were expelled from the neighbouring kingdom of Bungo, where they had been
tolerated on account of the high esteem entertained by the king for one of their number, Father
Gregory de Cerpides.   His death was the signal
for their banishment and the destruction of their
churches.   In the kingdom of Firando also, in
the year 1611, three native Christians, Gasper, his
wife and son, were martyred, suffering with great
fortitude.   Such events clearly proved that a
persecution would probably soon commence,
though no one could foresee the terrific violence
of the tempest about to break over their heads.
Nor were supernatural signs wanting to fore-
shadow the same thing.   On cutting down a
tree, too old to bear good fruit, some Christians
were astonished to find in the centre a well-
fashioned cross, with the title over it written
in plain letters.   This was in the kingdom of
Omura, and another cross was afterwards discovered in a tree of the same kind, in the garden
belonging to the Church of All Saints in
Nagasaki.   These mysterious crosses were con-

sidered as supernatural warnings that the Church in Japan was about to drink of the chalice of her Crucified Lord.

———

CHAPTER III.

Outbreak of the Persecution. Martyrdom of Father Peter of the Assumption, O.S.F., and Father Baptist Tavora, S.J.

TAIKO-SAMA, who had crucified the proto-martyrs of Japan, died in 1598, and his death was followed by some years of civil war. " Power then passed into the hands of a man scarcely less able than himself, Ieyasu, in whom the office of Shogun (in abeyance since 1573) was restored, and who founded the Toku-gawa dynasty or Shogunate. A period of comparative peace and prosperity " (as described in the last chapter) " now ensued. . . . But the peace was of short duration ; it was only the prelude to one of the most awful persecutions ever recorded in the history of the Church." *

At first the Shogun was not actively hostile to Christianity and favoured the Jesuit bishop, Luiz Serqueyra, even receiving him in the city of Kyoto. A native Christian named Paul was one of his favourites and advisers, but falling under his

* L. C. Casartelli.

displeasure became the occasion of anger against the Christians in general.

But this was not the principal reason of the persecution. About this time an event most fatal to Christianity happened in the arrival of Dutch and English Protestants. These men, who hated the Catholic Church more bitterly than the heathen emperor himself, stirred up the persecution, during which they constantly assisted the enemies of the Faith. A Dutch vessel, commanded by an Englishman of the name of William Adams, was wrecked on the Japanese coast. Leave was granted to the crew to build another ship, but, in the meantime, the Spanish pilot was imprudently taking a survey of the coast, in order to construct charts. The Shogan, hearing this, asked Adams whether it was customary in Europe to allow foreigners to survey a country without leave of the govern-ment. Adams replied that such a proceeding would not be tolerated in Europe, and that the truth was, that the Spaniards wanted accurate charts of the Japanese coast in order to be able to subdue the whole country and take possession of it for the Spanish crown, as they had already done in the Philippine Islands. It is well known, also, added this English Protestant, that the religious who have come into Japan under pre-tence of preaching the gospel, are merely spies of their government, sent to incite the people

against their rulers. For this reason the Princes
of Germany, the Kings of England, Denmark,
Sweden, and the Republic of Holland, have expelled the religious from their dominions as the
only means of preserving the public peace.
These representations—prompted partly by commercial jealousy, partly by hatred of the Catholic
faith—violently inflamed the anger of the
Shogan against Christianity. The result was an
edict commanding all missionaries to quit the
empire, forbidding any Japanese to profess
Christianity under pain of death, and ordering
all the churches to be destroyed. This edict
was carried out with greater rigour in some provinces than in others, according to the dispositions of the kings and governors, but everywhere
its effects were very soon felt. The King of
Figen—who had for several years highly favoured
the Friars-Preachers, and still entertained the utmost respect for their disinterested charity—dared
not brave the anger of the Shogan, and so
ordered them to quit his dominions. They
collected their beloved Christians in the church
at Famamachi, and gave them the holy sacraments, exhorting them earnestly to remember the
promises of fidelity they had made to God.
Frequently their words were interrupted by the
sobs of their children and their own tears. It
was a sorrowful parting, but necessary in order
that they might still be able to help the Church,

and they promised to return in disguise to visit and encourage their flock. They then departed with heavy hearts, though full of confidence in God's protection and the prayers of His Holy Mother. Father John of the Angels disguised himself as a Japanese and went into the kingdom of Omura, to assist the deserted Christians there; while Fathers Alphonsus de Mena and Hyacinth Orphanel, still in their habits, journeyed together to Nagasaki. Shortly after their arrival several native Christians—members of the Confraternity of the Holy Rosary—were martyred by order of the governor, and though some of them were only children of tender age, they all bravely endured till the end. Many other members of the Confraternity accompanied them to the place of execution with lighted candles and rosaries in their hands, praying for the grace of perseverance. The religious of the different Orders had been driven out of all the provinces, as the Dominicans had been from Satsuma, Figen and others, and most of them had collected secretly in Nagasaki, though many had been sent to Macao and Manilla. Father Balthazar Fort, therefore, compassionating the deserted condition of the poor Christians, sent the friars, concealed as Japanese, into the various kingdoms of the empire, to confirm the faith of the converts, to console them, and to give them the holy sacraments. He himself went into Arima and

Macusa, and other parts, assisting the Christians, who were very numerous, and afterwards, going by night to Famamachi, in the kingdom of Figen, he found the Dominican church not destroyed, and said Mass there, to the extreme joy of the Christians. In passing through the kingdom of Bungo he was in a district where there was no Christian house, but was informed that at some little distance he would find a Christian lady whose husband was a heathen. The lady of the house was absent on his arrival, but the infidel husband not only received him with civility but went in search of his wife, at the same time begging the Father to remain seated near the fire, as the cold was intense. Whilst awaiting his return the daughter approached with an infant son, and told him secretly that she was a Christian and desired to confess, and to have the child baptized. Her religion was a secret carefully hidden from her heathen parent, so Father Balthazar heard her confession and baptized the child, still standing at the fire. Passing by the same place a year after, he found that the little child had died, and its salvation through baptism gave him great joy and consolation.

Before the emperor's decree for the destruction of the Christian churches was carried out in Nagasaki, public prayers were offered up to obtain grace to sustain the sufferings which were about to fall upon the faithful. Penitential processions were formed, the first one starting from the Dominican church. It was attended by an immense number of Christians of all classes, wearing white tunics and bearing lighted candles in their hands, many with crowns of thorns on their heads, and disciplining themselves to blood. After a fervent sermon from Father Thomas of the Holy Ghost, the procession issued from the church, the Litanies being sung with great devotion. Similar processions were afterwards formed in the churches of the Augustinian, the Jesuit, and the Franciscan fathers. The Forty Hours Prayer before the Blessed Sacrament also took place in the Dominican and Jesuit churches, together with the administration of the holy sacraments. Thus did the Church prepare for the contest. Afterwards the governor of Nagasaki commanded the religious to depart from the empire, but instead they disguised themselves and separated into the different provinces to aid the Christians in secret. For nearly three years after the publication of the edict against the Church, it was nowhere enforced to the letter— especially when the emperor's attention was engrossed by a war in which he became involved. During this war the religious in Nagasaki began to show themselves again without fear, and to say Mass in the Christian houses almost as publicly as when they possessed churches. At this time also the Dominican Fathers were more zealous than ever in spreading the devotion of the Holy Rosary and enrolling thousands of the native Christians in the Confraternity. In some places all the Christians became members, as in a town called Myne in the kingdom of Arima.

The Shogan who had begun the persecution was succeeded by a man who hated Christianity with still greater bitterness, and was determined that the decrees against it should be enforced. Many native Christians had been already put to death in different places, but the religious had only been ordered to leave the country—a command they had disobeyed. In the year 1617, therefore, the apostate King of Omura apprehended two priests in his province who were labouring secretly among the Christians, and cast them into prison. They were Father Peter of the Assumption, a Franciscan, and Father John Baptist Tavora, of the Society of Jesus. Shortly after, both these religious glorified God by a martyr's death, being beheaded on the 2nd of May, 1617, and their names head the list of those two hundred and five beatified in July, 1867, by Pius IX. This brings us to the history of the Dominican proto-martyr in Japan, Blessed Alphonsus Naverette.

———

CHAPTER IV.

*Life and Martyrdom of Blessed Father
Alphonsus Navarette.*

WHEN the martyrdom of Peter of the
Assumption and John Baptist Tavora
took place in Omura, Father Alphonsus
Navarette was in Nagasaki, having succeeded
Father Balthazar Fort as vicar provincial of the
Order in Japan. This father, whose glorious death
for Christ is now to be related, was a Spaniard
of noble family, born in the city of Valladolid,
where he took the habit of our holy Father St.
Dominic in the Priory of S. Paul. Four years
afterwards he was sent to the Province of the
Holy Rosary, in the Philippine Islands, where
for some years he laboured amongst the natives,
and then travelled to Europe to obtain a fresh
supply of fathers for that distant mission. On
his return he was selected for the Japanese
mission, and entered the empire, with one
companion, in 1611. He had accompanied
Father Hyacinth Orphanel to the city of Miako,
the capital city of the whole empire, and therefore the most perilous for a missionary. He
was a man of great courage and enterprising

D

spirit, which was directed by the love of God to the benefit of souls. The virtue for which he was chiefly distinguished was extreme tender-hearted charity. This extended even to the inferior animals, to which he was always gentle and kind, remembering that saying of the Holy Ghost, *Novit justus jumentorum suorum animas : viscera autem impiorum crudelia ;* " The just man regardeth the lives of his beasts : but the tender mercies of the wicked are cruel." * His charity made him a true father to the poor ; he was ever at their service, giving all the alms within his power, and doing everything he could to relieve their temporal distress.

For sinners also he had a tender love, bearing with them, comforting and assisting them by his words and prayers, and thus leading large numbers back to God. He was ready at all hours to hear the confessions of the poor, pre-ferring them to the rich, who, he said, could easily find confessors, and such was his assiduity and zeal that he hardly spared time for necessary sleep and food. The sick also moved his loving heart to deep compassion, and his attention to their spiritual and temporal necessities was un-remitting. In Japan the poor, especially those afflicted with disease, were little cared for, and thus Father Alphonsus found ample field for his charity. In conjunction with the fathers of S.

* *Prov.* xii. 10.

Francis and S. Augustine, he founded a confraternity for the benefit of the sick poor.
Sometimes the fathers found the aged and sick
poor lying deserted on the wayside, and their
charity then prompted them to provide necessaries
for their bodies and instruction and baptism for
their souls. Another work which Father Alphonsus had very closely at heart was the baptism
of the numerous foundling children left by their
inhuman parents to perish by cold or hunger or
to fall a prey to wild beasts. These he used to
collect and baptize, and give them to be nursed
by charitable Christians. Just before his death
he wrote to Paul Garrucho, a Spanish captain,
begging him for the love of God to continue his
alms for the foundlings. " May Jesus be ever in
your soul," he wrote, " and give you eternal life.
Do not forget your alms for the little foundlings,
for thus you do God a great service. I write
this on a desert island, where I await my
death."

Another of his works was the erection of the
Confraternity of the Holy Name of Jesus in
Nagasaki, by which the faith and piety of the
Christians was greatly increased. All these
works of charity Father Alphonsus united to an
intense love of prayer and a strict observance
of his rule. When we hear that he effected all
these things when his health was weak and
frequently caused him much suffering, it is

evident that he was a truly mortified and self-denying religious. This virtuous life was crowned by a martyr's death, and, says Father Diego Advarte, the Priory of S. Paul, which had already given so many learned scholars to the Province of the Holy Rosary, did more than all besides by sending this glorious martyr.

This being Father Alphonsus Navarette's character, it is not surprising that he was deeply moved when he heard of the martyrdom of Peter of the Assumption and John Baptist de Tavora in Omura. He rejoiced indeed at their victory and felt a strong desire to share their happiness, but at the same time he heartily deplored the deserted condition of the Christians of that province, who were now left as sheep without pastors, and some of whom, yielding to cowardice, had imitated their king's example and apostatized, though most remained stedfast in their faith. Father Alphonsus did not content himself with mere sorrow; he considered the time had come for bold action, and under the inspiration of the Holy Ghost he determined to go into Omura to succour the poor Christians. On May 24, 1617, the eve of Corpus Christi, he determined to put this plan into execution. It was equivalent to offering himself for martyrdom, since the governor of Omura had given the strictest orders to his servants to search for missionaries that they might be put to death.

After this decision he asked a native Christian named Paul, who had for a long time acted as his catechist, whether he would dare to accompany him into the kingdom of Omura to rescue the bodies of Father Peter of the Assumption and Father John Baptist de Tavora from the hands of the heathen. " I have determined," said the Father, "to go into Omura and assist the Christians there, while at the same time I shall reproach the king with his base apostasy, reminding him that he has been guilty of an enormous crime, for which he has merited eternal punishment." Paul eagerly begged to accompany him, to share the dangers of his bold design. Gaspar Ficogiro also, who had for a long time sheltered Father Alphonsus in his house, entreated to be allowed to join them, and his request was granted.

Before setting out on his journey Father Alphonsus wrote the following letter to the friars in Japan :

"Jesus be in your hearts, and give you His Holy Spirit.

" You are well aware, Reverend Fathers, to what danger Christianity is now exposed, how it every day loses ground, and how necessary it is to support the Christians by a bold example. Therefore I entreat you by the bowels of the mercy of our good Jesus, to be true children of our holy Father S. Dominic, and to live in

great peace and brotherly love with the other
religious Orders. I am going to Omura to
comfort and strengthen the Christians, whom
the blood of two martyrs has disposed to receive
much fruit from our ministry. May the Divine
Majesty direct my steps to His glory. As I may
be cast into prison, I appoint Father Francis de
Morales as vicar in my place. If I have the
happiness of confessing the faith by martyrdom,
you must choose another vicar provincial as
our constitutions direct. I beg and implore you
to forget the bad example I have given you,
whether in office or as a private religious.
Remember me in your sacrifices and prayers.
Paul desires to sacrifice himself in the service
of the Lord, and to accompany me, so that
I commit his wife and children to your care.
Never forget the work of the foundlings; may it
prosper and be the salvation of all those poor
little creatures.

"BROTHER ALPHONSUS NAVARETTE.

"May 24, 1617.   Feast of the Translation of our
Holy Father S. Dominic."

The two who had offered to accompany
Father Alphonsus were both laymen, and he
reflected that it would be necessary to have
a priest to assist him in hearing confessions.
He therefore proposed the plan to Father
Ferdinand of St. Joseph, the vicar provincial
of the Order of S. Augustine in Japan.

He was a religious of great holiness of life, remarkable for humility, zeal, and a tender compassion for the souls in purgatory. He constantly said Mass for them, refusing alms for the Masses, that he might offer them for his favourite intention. Each morning he went to confession before celebrating Mass, and then used to hear Mass, and sometimes two or three in thanksgiving. For three years he had been the only member of his Order in Japan, and during that time he had lived with the Friars Preachers as if he had been a Dominican. Father Alphonsus was his confessor, and he had taken a vow of obedience to him while living thus far from his own superiors. These two religious, though very different in natural character, were very intimate friends, and in Nagasaki lived close together and constantly consulted each other. At first Father Ferdinand's humility shrank from Father Alphonsus's bold design, and he feared that so glorious a work was above his grace. They prayed, therefore, that the Divine Will might be manifested on the subject, and whilst doing so Father Alphonsus was seen lifted up in the air, his face shining with a brilliant light. After this Father Ferdinand put himself into his friend's hands, to be at his disposal, as if he were his own superior. "If I had a superior here," said this good religious, "I should throw myself blindly at his feet and obey; not having one here, I promise the like submission to your commands." " In the name of God then, father," was the reply, "come with me to this work."

This was decided on the feast of Corpus Christi, and both the fathers said Mass that morning with unusual devotion, begging the guidance of the Holy Spirit. Then Father Ferdinand wrote a letter to the Dominicans of Japan and the Augustinians of Manilla, explaining the circumstances of his resolution, and begging pardon with great humility for not having worn the habit of S. Augustine with becoming holiness, and praying that God would send worthy apostles into Japan. Before starting on their journey the two friends consulted Father Francis de Morales, a religious of the highest learning, prudence and virtue, who, after hearing the admirable reasons urged for their project, which he at first judged to be rash, gave at length a favourable answer and his blessing to Father Alphonsus, who had humbly cast himself at his feet. " Perhaps," he said, "you may languish long in prison." "We are ready to suffer for Christ," replied Father Alphonsus, "and to endure a long martyrdom for His sake." Father Francis promised to say twelve Masses if they were taken in Omura, and begged the two apostles to remember him when they entered the presence of God.

They found it impossible to leave Nagasaki

secretly during the day, so they waited till night near the resting-place of some martyrs, begging their prayers and assistance. Then they journeyed forth and reached a neighbouring village, where they found many Christians most anxious to receive the holy sacraments. For four days they remained here, working incessantly, hearing confessions, instructing and baptizing the whole day and the greater part of the night. The chief man of this town, bearing an office somewhat equivalent to that of mayor in an English town, was an apostate Christian, and only the week before had captured Father Peter of the Assumption and delivered him into the hands of the king.

This man was astonished at the boldness displayed by the two fathers, and, touched by grace, he fell on his knees and begged to be admitted once more into the Church and to the benefit of the sacraments. This proves that Father Alphonsus was guided by the Holy Ghost, when he said that the time had arrived when a bold example of Christian courage was necessary. Before the arrival of the fathers the Christians of this place had become faint-hearted and almost ready to yield to their persecutors, but encouraged by their example all their fervour returned ; they flocked publicly to confession, and invited the friars into their houses, though well aware that this placed their lives in imminent danger. It very soon became impossible for the fathers to conceal themselves, owing to the vast numbers of the faithful who flocked from all sides, overjoyed to see a priest and earnestly demanding the sacraments. No building could be found spacious enough to hold the crowds desirous of hearing Mass, so that the fathers celebrated under the trees in a field near the village, the holy Sacrifice being followed by a sermon. On leaving the place the *Salve Regina* and Litanies were sung, and then the missionaries solemnly blessed the kneeling crowd of the faithful, leaving with them for their comfort and instruction the *Lives of the Saints* and Father Lewis of Granada's *Sinner's Guide*, which had been well translated into Japanese. Since, owing to the persecution, no missionaries had been able to enter Omura for a long time, many of the confessions involved considerable difficulties, and many were discovered to have apostatized, so that Father Alphonsus, as superior of the Order, sent word to Father Francis de Morales to choose two fathers to visit these same places in order to finish and confirm the work thus happily begun. For three years the friars had been obliged to disguise themselves as laymen, sometimes as Japanese, sometimes as Spanish merchants, but now they considered that the moment had arrived in which they should assume their religious habits and wear their proper tonsure. The joy with which they made these changes was not greater than that of the poor Christians when they saw once more those beloved habits; they crowded round, weeping and kissing the scapular with great reverence and devotion. Scenes such as these took place in each village through which the two religious passed.

One morning after Mass a large band of soldiers, many of whom were apostate Christians, arrived with orders from the king of Omura to capture the fathers and bring them at once to the capital city. These officers, though they had not the courage to disobey their master, were most civil to the fathers, begging their pardon humbly for taking them prisoners, but saying that their lives would be forfeited if they refused. The religious answered that for themselves nothing was more desirable, though they grieved for the sin that was thus committed. Father Alphonsus then gave the following letter to one of the officers, charging him strictly to deliver it to the apostate king.

" The superior of the Order of S. Augustine and the superior of the Order of S. Dominic have come to aid the suffering Christians, having heard with great wonder of the martyrdom of certain priests, a crime very great for a heathen to commit, but for one who has been baptized most terribly grievous. Filled with sorrow, therefore, we have come, Sire, to warn you to repent of this crime, to confess it, and to endeavour to make your subjects do the same, as far as they are guilty ; otherwise we warn you that you will be lost in hell for ever, without any hope of release. For this reason we send you this letter."

Then Gaspar, the host of Father Alphonsus, stept boldly forward, and reproaching the soldiers for their cowardice, offered himself to accompany the fathers. "Take me also," he cried ; " I have disobeyed the emperor, for three years I have sheltered a priest in my house. Take me also to martyrdom." His time had not yet arrived—later his desire was granted ; but now the soldiers would not allow either him or Paul, the faithful catechist, to accompany the religious. Much did the priests desire to tarry till the next day, that they might again celebrate the holy Sacrifice and hear the remaining confessions, but the officers would not consent, and insisted on their immediate embarkation for the city of Omura. No words can describe the scene of enthusiasm among the faithful as the religious were conducted to the boats. They thronged the road, having collected from all parts in great numbers ; they wept and sobbed aloud, asking for a parting benediction from their beloved fathers. In vain did the soldiers endeavour to disperse them by blows with clubs and lances ; they pressed around kissing the martyrs' hands, and cutting off pieces of their scapulars and habits, so that "when they had embarked," says an old writer, "they scarce had habits to cover them."

Many of the faithful followed the fathers in boats, determined to remain near them as long as possible, and perhaps hoping to share their crowns as martyrs. Those left behind stood gazing at the boat that was carrying away to a cruel death those whom they so greatly loved and venerated, and the grief of their hearts breaking out in words, they filled the air with their lamentations. Their distress was the only thing that afflicted the martyrs, who rejoiced exceedingly that they were accounted worthy to suffer for Christ.

The fathers arrived in Omura at midnight, and the king gave immediate orders for their execution. He was greatly afflicted when he saw them, and remorse seems to have troubled his soul; but he loved the world dearly, and justly feared the displeasure of the emperor if he spared the missionaries. His desire was to conceal the whole affair from the people, and he therefore ordered the execution to take place on a desert island called Ufuxima. The Christians, however, followed, desirous to make their confessions, and amongst them were two relatives of the king—Magdalen and Marina. To Magdalen Father Alphonsus gave a little image of our Lady, which she hung round her neck and promised constantly to wear.

To avoid this concourse of people the soldiers once more embarked with the fathers and sailed to another island called Amegora, where they hoped to be able quietly to despatch their victims according to the king's command. Permission was granted Father Alphonsus to walk over the island before the sentence was executed, his desire being to see if there were any concealed Christians who might thus have an opportunity of approaching the sacraments. Ascending a hill in the centre of the little island, he raised his eyes to heaven, and lifting his cross high in the air sung with a loud voice the praises of the most High God, pouring out his soul in sighs of love and of desire to shed his blood for Christ. On his return he discovered a cavern in the side of the hill, in which a number of Christians were collected. After hearing their confessions he exhorted them to perseverance and left them comforted and strengthened, and then, returning to the soldiers, delivered himself joyfully to their custody.

Finding that the Christians persisted in following them, the soldiers carried the fathers to another island, called Coguchi, and here they found the bodies of the two late martyrs, Peter of the Assumption and John Baptist of Tavora, which the king had ordered to be transported to this distant island, owing to the veneration paid by the Christians to their relics. The soldiers in charge of the sacred remains of these martyrs had orders to execute a youthful Japanese, named Leo, who had constantly served Mass for Father John Baptist. To escape the determined vigilance of the Christians the soldiers again sailed with their captives at midnight for a still more distant island, and thinking that now at last they must be alone they commanded the fathers to prepare for immediate death. But neither was this the place chosen by God for the sacrifice. Father Alphonsus recognised some Christians disguised as sailors, and asked them to fashion for him a rude cross with two pieces of wood, that he might die with the sacred symbol before his eyes. Seeing this, the soldiers once more delayed their martyrdom, and sought a yet more remote spot, called the island of Tocaxima. Here they ordered the holy men to kneel down, a command they obeyed with the utmost joy, seeing that the long-desired moment had arrived. Alphonsus was in the centre, on his right hand knelt Father Ferdinand, on his left the youthful Leo. Father Ferdinand was the first martyr. Kneeling for a time in prayer, he kissed the sword which was to send his soul to eternal rest, and then, taking his rosary in one hand and a blessed candle in the other, he bowed his head to the blow. The stroke descended, and the martyr was with God.

Father Alphonsus was the next victim. Clothed in the white habit of our Lady, this true son of S. Dominic knelt in joyful expectation of the moment in which he could complete his sacrifice by giving his life for Christ. His countenance shone with a joy that was the reflection of his soul, as if a ray from the heaven to which he was speeding had fallen upon him before the time ; his right hand grasped the cross, and in his left were his beads and the blessed taper of the Rosary Confraternity. The last words he uttered were those he had so often chanted in his convent choir during the weekly office of the departed, " *I will please the Lord in the land of the living.*" * Perhaps the heavenly beauty of the figure before them unnerved the executioner, for the first stroke only mutilated without killing the sufferer. He fell backwards on the ground, his eyes looking up to heaven, where his heart had already taken refuge. The third stroke finished the work, and S. Dominic numbered another martyr among his children. Leo, the youthful native, received the palm of victory after a single blow.

Thus were representatives of the four religious orders which had sent missionaries to Japan martyred almost together. But God, who has

* *Ps.* cxiv. 9.

raised them all to glory, was pleased to unite them still more closely upon earth. The heathen, as was mentioned above, had carried away the relics of Father Peter of the Assumption and Father John Baptist, to prevent the concourse of the faithful at their tomb. They now opened the coffins containing the remains of these two martyrs, and with them they enclosed the bodies of Father Alphonsus and Father Ferdinand. Then they tied heavy weights to each, and cast them into the deep waters of the sea. In one coffin sank the relics of the Jesuit, John Baptist de Tavora, and the Friar Preacher, Alphonsus Navarette ; in the other, those of the Augustinian, Ferdinand of S. Joseph, and the Friar Minor, Peter of the Assumption. Thus did God show how much He is pleased with peace, harmony, mutual support, and brotherly love between those who, though under different rules and forming different divisions of one apostolic army, are still united in one faith, one work, and in the love that makes them yearn to shed their blood for one and the same Lord.

The executioners to whom the duty of despatching the martyrs had been committed, were for the most part apostate Christians, who greatly disliked their task but were afraid to disobey the king. So much reverence did they entertain for the martyrs, that when their hated duty had been performed, they dipped cloths in the

E

blood and preserved them, with the habits, as precious relics, saying that they trusted God would give them one day the grace of conversion through the prayers of His servants. The sword used at the execution was afterwards sold to the Christians for 150 crowns, and sent to the Dominicans of Manilla.

This glorious martyrdom took place on the octave day of Corpus Christi, June 1, 1617, and five years later, by command of the Sacred Congregation of Rites, the Archbishop of Manilla made the enquiries necessary to enable the Holy See to proceed to the beatification of the martyrs. In 1668 the same Sacred Congregation declared that the process was valid, and that death had been inflicted out of hatred to religion. In 1863 Pius IX. authorized new investigations to decide whether death had been accepted by the martyrs for the love of Jesus Christ and to bear witness to the truth. The answer being favourable, the four martyrs were solemnly beatified on July 7, 1867.

CHAPTER V.

Capture of Father Thomas of the Holy Ghost. Heroism of Native Members of the Holy Rosary.

WITHOUT a direct movement of the Holy Spirit, the bold way in which Father Alphonsus braved the anger of the king and really offered himself for martyrdom, might have been condemned as a rash tempting of God. That the design did proceed from the action of the Holy Ghost, who filled the martyr's soul with the gift of fortitude, is made evident by the heroic courage he displayed at his death, and by the wonderful benefit which his example proved to the persecuted Church. Some of the good effected during the journey to Omura has already been described, but the work of grace did not end there. His death seemed to pour an invigorating spirit of life into the whole Church of Japan. Fervour was everywhere renewed. The faint-hearted grew courageous, and the spirit of Christian heroism inspired the faithful with a desire to show that they also could suffer and die for their Lord. A great battle has sometimes been decided by the valour of one man, whose example has re-animated the sinking courage of his fellow-soldiers. The same happened in this Christian warfare.

But, besides this natural effect, an act of self-sacrifice so sublime, prompted simply by zeal for God's honour, could not fail to draw down the richest graces from His Majesty. Nagasaki was the first place to feel the good effects of this martyrdom. Those who had before been afraid to receive the missionaries into their houses, now offered them hospitality. The priests were besieged on all sides by Christians asking for the sacraments with great devotion, and some even went to search for the relics of the martyrs, venerating the place of their sacrifice, and trying to recover the bodies from the deep sea. Amongst these was Andrew Tocuan, son of the Christian governor of Nagasaki, whose glorious death will presently be related. Another good result of Father Alphonsus's example was the heroic way in which many Japanese suffered martyrdom, some of whom had before denied their faith. Thus an apostate, named Dominic Yamaguchi, repented at the news of Father Alphonsus's martyrdom and incurred the special hatred of the persecutors by openly proclaiming his faith and encouraging the other Christians. He was beheaded with his wife and family.

But the most striking effect of all was the

vast change which took place in the kingdom of Omura, which, through the evil example of the king and the absence of the missionaries, had become like a dreary desert, but now resembled a delightful garden, bearing the choicest flowers of Christian virtue. Father Francis de Morales, who had succeeded Blessed Alphonsus as vicar provincial, selected Fathers Thomas of the Holy Ghost and John of the Angels to undertake the hazardous task of completing the good work begun in that kingdom. They were accompanied by Father Apolinarius Franco, a Friar Minor, and Brother Mance of S. Thomas, a professed choir religious of the Dominican Order, who, being a Japanese, was well qualified to assist the fathers as catechist. The good resulting from this mission was immense. Apostates were reconciled in large numbers to the Church, the faithful were fortified by the sacraments, and the work begun by Alphonsus Navarette and Peter of the Assumption was finished and confirmed. Many of the poor Christians, deprived for so long of teachers, had fallen, through ignorance and the persuasion of the bonzes, into superstitious and idolatrous customs without intending completely to deny their faith. For more than a month the good work continued without interruption, but on July 7 the Franciscan Father Apolinarius was taken prisoner with several Japanese that

were assisting him, and fifteen days later Father
Thomas of the Holy Ghost and Brother Mance
fell also into the power of the persecutors. Father
Thomas had crossed over to an island inhabited
by numerous Christians, and so public did his
presence become by the crowds desirous to hear
Mass and approach the sacraments, that information was sent by the bonzes to the king, who
gave immediate orders for his arrest. Paul
Nangasci — the native catechist who had so
bravely accompanied Alphonsus Navarette and
offered himself for martyrdom — obtained the
accomplishment of his desires, being apprehended with Father Thomas. They were all
confined together in prison at a place called
Satsuta, about six miles from the town of Cuxima,
in the kingdom of Omura.

It seems marvellous that Father John of the
Angels did not also fall into the persecutors'
power. He was employed in the same ministry
as Father Thomas, and thinking it impossible he
could escape and therefore judging disguise to
be useless, he openly wore his religious habit.
Still it was not God's will he should be taken,
and he continued his labour among the people
unmolested. In all these things the finger of
God's Providence is plainly visible—allowing His
servants to be taken by their enemies, or to escape
dangers the most imminent, as His glory and the
advantage of Holy Church required. This is

apparent also as to Gaspar Fisogiro, who had accompanied Father Alphonsus Navarette, and begged the soldiers to apprehend him, stating that he had for two years harboured missionaries in his house, thus breaking the royal command. In spite of these bold words the soldiers had refused to arrest him, and his life had been given to him against his will. But now the appointed moment had arrived. Orders were sent by the king for the immediate imprisonment of all who had sheltered missionaries in their houses, and Gaspar was seized in company with Andrew Gioscinda, who had lodged Father Ferdinand of S. Joseph.

In prison they gave themselves entirely to exercises of devotion and penance, being sometimes privately visited by Fathers of the Order and thus receiving the holy sacraments. On the last day of September they were again taken to their own homes, and everything was done to shake their constancy, but the valiant confessors despised the threats as well as the promises of the heathen.

Seeing that it was impossible to make them abandon their religion, the persecutors carried them to a desert island, called Tacabuco, and then cutting off their heads threw their bodies into the sea. This martyrdom took place just after midnight, so that they obtained their crown on October 1, the feast of the Holy Rosary, a circumstance which afforded them great pleasure, as

they were both fervent members of the Rosary Confraternity and loving sons of the Queen of Heaven.
Gaspar especially was a great benefactor to the
Order, having for a considerable time risked his
property and life by affording the Fathers of S.
Dominic a shelter under his roof.   Three friars
were actually lodging in his house when the guards
came to seize him, but they escaped unperceived.
For the reward of his charity he wears the martyr's
crown.   Andrew had been educated from his
childhold in a school conducted by Jesuit fathers,
and was an example of Christian virtue.   These
two martyrs are amongst those beatified by Pius
IX., but many others belonging to the Confraternity
suffered in a similar way, though they have not received the honour of being beatified.

Amongst these the story of Linus Xirobioye is
remarkable.   This man had been converted to
Christianity, but when the king of Omura, in whose
court he was a distinguished favourite, apostatized,
Linus followed his master's example, abjured his
faith, and was employed by the king to persecute
the Christians.   When Father Peter of the Assumption was in prison with Father John Baptist de
Tavora, Almighty God by a miracle of His divine
compassion touched the apostate's heart with grace,
and he was reconciled to the Church before the
death of the two fathers.   His conversion was not
public, and he continued high in the king's favour
and holding an influential position, which enabled

him to be of immense assistance to the Christians. Many who had become apostates were converted by his means. After the imprisonment of Father Thomas of the Holy Ghost the king went to consult with the emperor as to the way of treating the martyrs, and during his absence left Linus Xirobioye as governor in his place. This was joyful news for the Christians. By the consent and advice of the governor they flocked in crowds to the prison, and the fathers were constantly employed in hearing their confessions, confirming their faith, and receiving back those who had through fear abandoned their religion. On the king's return the bonzes, who had watched the governor's conduct with a jealous eye, openly accused him of being a Christian. He boldly acknowledged the truth of the accusation, and the enraged king sent him to immediate execution on November 4, 1617.

After this the imprisonment of missionaries became more strict, the guards were doubled, and orders were given that no one should be allowed to hold communication with them. A brave youth named Andrew one day presented himself before the prison and asked permission to speak to the fathers. His request was refused, and he was examined as to his religion. Fortified by the Holy Spirit, he proclaimed himself a Christian, and said that he had journeyed through the different villages of Omura, comforting the Christians and distributing good books among them for their consolation

and instruction.   The king gave orders that he
should be stripped of his clothes and confined in a
cage of strong reeds, with nothing to protect him
from the cold.   It was November, and the cold in
Japan during that month is intense.   For a whole
month the heroic youth bore his torture, the same
God, says Father Adverte, who tempered the fiery
heat of the furnace into which the three Jewish
youths were cast, enabling this Japanese youth to
endure the insufferable cold to which he was exposed.   The fire of divine love, which burnt in his
soul, must have supplied his body with heat, as we
read of Blessed Sebastian of Apparizio, the Franciscan lay brother, who was sometimes obliged to
tear away his habit and lie in the frost the whole
night, in order to cool the unbearable flame of love
that tortured his breast.   After this wonderful imprisonment Andrew, who protested that never had
he enjoyed such happiness as during that month,
was liberated, and continued as before—distributing
books and consoling his fellow-Christians, telling
them that nothing could be more delightful than to
suffer for Christ.

During the time of comparative liberty afforded
them by the favour of the Christian governor, the
fathers had enjoyed the unspeakable consolation of
being able to offer daily the holy Sacrifice of the
Mass—the necessary things being supplied by the
faithful, who had free access to the prison.   This
was reported to the king, and orders were sent that

everything used for any sacred rite, as well as every picture and religious emblem, should be taken away from the prisoners, who were in future to be tightly bound in a cruel manner common in Japan, with cords passing round their hands, shoulders, and neck. For a considerable time they were every day expecting the end to come, but it was God's will to prove their constancy by a lingering martyrdom of nearly six years duration.

Before closing this chapter some mention must be made of a noble-hearted native Christian named John Nizemon, who was a devout member of the Rosary Confraternity, and thus closely connected with the Order of S. Dominic. He was a subject of the king of Omura, and much given to idolatrous practices, when he was unsettled in his mind by the exhortations of Linus Xirobioye, who was afterwards governor. Going to Nagasaki, Nizemon listened most attentively to the instructions of the missionaries, and getting a Japanese catechism, studied the Christian doctrine with the careful attention a subject so momentous deserved. For some time he was tormented by many doubts and difficulties (a rare thing for a heathen), but being really desirous to discover the true way of salvation, God came to his assistance, and bestowed upon him the gift of Faith. He became a fervent Christian, and often visited the Fathers Thomas and Apolinarius in their prison at Satsuta. The king, discovering this, confined him to his own house as a prison, surrounding it with guards, and on December '23 the sentence of death was announced to him.   Joyfully he received the tidings, and promising to be mindful of all his friends when he had obtained the martyr's crown, he kept silence during the time that preceded his death, speaking only to God and forgetting everything on earth. On Christmas day, 1617, the sentence was carried out by his head being struck off.   His relics were secured at great risk by his fellow-members of the Rosary Confraternity.   The reader can easily imagine what solid comforts events like these must have afforded to the captive fathers, and that they stood in sore need of spiritual support and consolation the following chapter will clearly manifest.

CHAPTER VI.

The   Prisons   of   Satsula.   Father   John   of   S. Dominic.   His   Death.   Imprisonment   of Father   Francis   de   Morales   and   Father Alphonsus   de   Mena.

WHEN we hear of the heroic confessors of the faith in Japan being confined, many of them for long periods of time, in prison, awaiting their final triumph, we must not imagine them living in a commodious building like a modern jail. The prisons of the sixteenth and seventeenth centuries were places of terrible suffering even in Europe. In our own time a criminal, however abominable his crime, is treated with the utmost humanity, and though suffering loss of liberty, is confined in a well ventilated cell, scrupulously clean and well warmed, and furnished with every necessary for the health of the inmates.

But the "prisons" of Satsuta were by no means of this type. In Japan permanent buildings for confining malefactors were, two hundred years ago, unknown. Places were constructed as necessity required, and for the Christian prisoners part of an open field had been enclosed with thick stakes, forming a kind palisade with no roof, and nothing to protect the sufferers from the cutting blasts and biting frosts of the Japanese winter. With scarcely sufficient clothes to cover them, they were obliged to seek what repose they could upon the bare ground. To all this was added the torment of hunger—their food, scanty in allowance, consisting of rice boiled in water, without anything more solid to support them. Often they were tightly bound with cords in a way that caused intense and constant suffering. These cords, sometimes small and cutting, were bound round the neck, breast and arms; and the hands tied together brought the elbows almost into contact, and in this way were they led from place to place, and to the stake or the block on the day of execution.

It was almost miraculous that they survived these intense sufferings, for this was only their first winter, and five years had to pass before the hour of release. On their first Christmas day in confinement, in 1617, they were able to say Mass, which they did to their unspeakable comfort, and in the most secret possible manner. Christians from without had supplied them with requisites at their own imminent risk.

After this it is not wonderful that one priest died in this prison. Father John of S. Dominic had not been very long in the empire before his imprisonment. He was a Spaniard by birth, and took the habit of our holy Father S. Dominic in the renowned convent of S. Stephen in Salamanca, and after making considerable progress in piety and learning, he was urged by apostolic zeal to go to the province of the Philippines. With his companions he journeyed from Salamanca to Seville on foot, depending on the alms of the faithful, and in the same way he afterwards travelled on foot from Mexico to the port of Acapulco, this being then the common route to the Philippines. In these long and fatiguing journeys he displayed the patience, love of suffering, and genuine spirit of poverty which must characterize a missionary. On his arrival in Manilla his first care was to study the language of the Indian natives, among whom he laboured for some years with great energy and success. His superiors afterwards selected him to form one of a company sent to found a missionary province in Corea, from whence at the instigation of Father Francis de Morales he obtained leave to pass with Father Angelo Ferrer into Japan. They were learning the language at Nagasaki, when they were discovered, and conducted, together with two lay brothers, Thomas of the Rosary and John Nangoriki, to the prison of Satsuta. Their arrival was a great joy to Father Thomas of the Holy Ghost. *Laudate Dominum omnes gentes*, sang the new captives as they entered their prison, and with cheerful voice, in spite of his six months suffering, Father Thomas replied, *Quoniam confirmata est super nos misericordia ejus.*

God deals differently with His servants. It was His divine will to purify Father John of S. Dominic by spiritual sufferings, and then to call him to rest from the prison, while He reserved his companions for a more public confession. All his companions in the midst of their sufferings were supported by Divine consolations, but Father John endured an inward crucifixion. His humility made him tremble. He could not be convinced that one so unworthy would have the grace to die a martyr. Naturally of a timorous nature, he feared his sins might render him unfit for so glorious a triumph. His companions tried their utmost to console him, reminding him with

what fortitude the Holy Ghost had filled him
when standing before the governor of Nagasaki
after his capture, and how then, when asked who
he was, he had· answered boldly, " A religious
and a son of S. Dominic." They exhorted him
to trust ·in God without fear, since He ever helps
those who mistrust themselves. These comforting
words could not altogether reassure the humble
religious, who was being purified by the with-
drawal of spiritual consolations. A letter he
wrote to the prior of the convent at Manilla
breathes the same spirit. His bodily strength
could not withstand this combined suffering of
soul and body, and he fell dangerously ill. No
relief was allowed him in his sickness. Stretched
on the ground, his food was still only rice, and
medicine was forbidden. His only consolation
was the tender compassion of his brethren, who
watched over him with the utmost love, doing for
his soul what they were unable to do for his
bodily relief. In their arms he expired, in most
holy dispositions, on March 19, 1619, the feast of
S. Joseph, just three months after his entry into
prison.

As he died from the sufferings endured in prison
for the faith, he was as truly a martyr as if he
had laid his head upon the block or given his
body to be burnt, and he was beatified with
Alphonsus Navarette by Pius IX. After his
death the companions of his prison cut off a

finger and a foot, which they preserved as most precious relics, his body being carried off by the infidels, to prevent the faithful paying it veneration. They tried to burn it, but in vain did they heap pile after pile of wood round the sacred remains; the fire respected its Maker's servant, and the body remained unconsumed. The heathens, fiercer than the flames, chopped it into pieces, which they threw into the sea.

While these events were happening in the prison of Satsuta, the enemies of the faith were not idle. The chief governor of Nagasaki, which is a town under the direct jurisdiction of the emperor, died about this time, and a man named Gonrocu, a bitter enemy of the Christian religion, was appointed in his place. Under the chief governor there were two officials of high authority acting as vice-governors, and one of these was a Christian named Anthony Toan, while his colleague was an apostate of the name of Feyzo. Anthony had a married son, named Andrew Tocuan, and in his house Father Francis Morales was concealed. Shortly after the appointment of the new governor, Feyzo was careful to lodge an information with him, that resulted in the capture of the missionary and the imprisonment of Anthony and Andrew, together with several other Christians. The officers entered the house while Father Francis was at dinner, and on account of the high esteem in which he was

F

held in the city, they apologized for being obliged to apprehend him, to which he replied joyfully that it was the most glorious day of his life, and the one he had longed for ever since his first arrival in Japan. Before departing he once more clothed himself in his religious habit, which he had been obliged to lay aside for the last five years. The guards conducted him to the same prison into which Father Alphonsus de Mena with his host, John Xoan, and several other native Christians had been thrown only the day before. Both these fathers were among the the first Dominicans that nearly twenty years before had landed in the empire of Japan, and ever since that time had incessantly laboured for the salvation of souls amid many privations and sufferings. Both were Spaniards. Father Francis was a native of Madrid and a son of the Priory of S. Paul in the city of Valladolid. After teaching philosophy for some time in the Priory of S. Gregory at Valladolid, he went to the Philippines, and when the first missionaries were sent to Japan he was fulfilling the office of Prior in the Convent of Manilla. His common exclamation to his brethren was : "Oh ! my brothers, how beautiful is the land of Japan." His labours in the empire have already been mentioned, especially when driven from the kingdom of Satsuma. Father Alphonsus de Mena was a cousin of Alphonsus Navarette, and was professed in the Priory of

S. Stephen in Salamanca. He also had done good service among the infidel natives of the Philippine Islands, and since entering Japan, as described elsewhere, had laboured in many provinces of the empire with indefatigable energy, till forced by the violence of the persecution to take shelter in Nagasaki. For some time he lived in Anthony Toan's house, visiting the Christians during the night, and returning before the light to his hiding-place ; and afterwards he had wandered from one place of concealment to another, in continual danger and suffering, which at last ended in his imprisonment.

For eight days the native Christians were consoled amidst the sufferings of the prison by the company of these two missionaries. Then they had to endure the sorrows of a separation, the two priests being conveyed, on Palm Sunday, to another prison, situated in an island belonging to the kingdom of Firando, about thirty leagues distance from Nagasaki. Although every precaution was employed to prevent the Christians from discovering the Fathers on their journey, the news of their departure got abroad, and the faithful crowded round the landing-place, begging with tears for the privilege of a parting blessing, and as the ship sailed they filled the air with their cries and lamentations.

The cruelties inflicted upon the two Fathers in their new prison was barbarous in the extreme. A public proclamation forbade any one, under pain of death, to supply them with water, food, clothes, or any other necessary of life. Their prison was very narrow and incommodious, with one small window, through which the sky alone was visible, and this miserable chamber was pervaded by a poisonous stench. The food supplied to the prisoners was barely sufficient to sustain life, consisting only of a little rice, or a soup of radish leaves, and sometimes, by way of luxury, a dried herring. To add to all these hardships, Father Alphonsus fell dangerously ill, and was at the same time overcome by a profound melancholy, which often assailed him when not actively engaged in the duties of the apostolate. God, however, did not desert His servant, whom He intended for a glorious triumph. The comfort derived from the presence and conversation of Father Francis Morales, the consolation they both enjoyed in being able to offer the Holy Sacrifice, and the earnest desire he felt to suffer a martyr's death, all combined to restore him to health. After enduring this martyrdom for five months, the two Fathers were confined in the still worse prison of Satsuta, where for three years more they lingered in patient suffering*.

* See Father Meynard's *Missions Dominicaines dans l'extrême Orient*, vol. i., p. 290.

CHAPTER VII.

The Rosarians of Japan.

THE wonderful effect of the devotion of the Holy Rosary in Japan has been already mentioned. During the persecution it became one of the strongest defences of the Faith, and as its mysteries taught Christians the great truths of religion, so also the graces obtained by its recital fortified them against the attacks of the persecutor. The Rosary was the solace and support of those lingering for years in prison ; it hung round the neck of the martyr burning at the stake, it was clasped in the dying grasp of those who were tortured or beheaded. Often, indeed, the persecutors deprived the poor Christians of their beads, but the mysteries and prayers of the Rosary were beyond their reach. It is due to these heroic members of the Dominican Confraternity, to enter into some detail about a few of their number, which, for lack of space, must serve as specimens of the rest. Father Francis Carrero published a work called *The Triumph of the Rosary in Japan*, which is full of examples of the heroic virtues displayed by the members. In proportion to the persecution God increased the devotion to the Rosary and the graces

bestowed by its means. Its wide diffusion through
the empire has already been mentioned. It was
everywhere known and loved, and in whole districts
nearly every Christian was a member. Of the two
hundred and five martyrs beatified by Pius IX.,
Father Boero mentions more than sixty as members
of the Rosary, besides all the Tertiaries and fathers
of the Order, who were of course inscribed in the
ranks of the Confraternity.

Among these Rosarians a noble family of Nagasaki deserves special mention, as sending up to God
the sweet odour of many virtues, and furnishing
numerous and heroic martyrs for the Faith. The
head of this illustrious family was Anthony Toan,
who was distinguished among his countrymen, not
only for his noble birth, but also for his talents and
mental accomplishments, which together with his
uprightness of character won him the confidence of
the emperor and the appointment of vice-governor
of Nagasaki. But he was a Christian, and had harboured missionaries in his house. For these crimes,
shortly after the appointment of Gonrocu as Governor, he was put to death, his wife sharing his
martyrdom. He had five sons named Andrew,
Francis, John, Peter, and Paul, all Christians, as
their names sufficiently testify. The three last-
named were beheaded for the faith shortly after
their father. Francis had been educated for the
priesthood, and for some time served a church in
Nagasaki, when hearing of a battle about to take

place in one part of the empire, he hastened to assist the dying Christian soldiers, and was himself killed in performing this office of charity. But the most illustrious martyr of the family was Andrew Tocuan, the host of Father Francis Morales, in whose house that father had been taken. He and his wife Mary were models of virtue to the whole city of Nagasaki. The Confraternity of the Rosary in that city was divided into two companies, and Andrew was the leader of the division for the men ; his wife was at the head of the women. They were both also members and zealous propagators of the Confraternity of the Holy Name of Jesus, and served God fervently amidst constant works of charity and self-denial, with frequent prayer and penance, in continual danger of death by sheltering the hunted missionaries. Andrew was the first to risk his life, by trying to recover the bodies of the martyrs out of deep reverence for their relics. When the officers seized Father Morales in his house, Andrew was absent, and his heroic wife, knowing her husband's desire to suffer for Christ, overcame her natural feelings and sent for him, that his long cherished hopes might be realized. Great was his exultation when he found the time had come, and he was impatient to reach his prison. In consideration of his high rank the satellites desired to carry him to prison in a closed chair, but he refused, saying that to walk to prison bound for

Christ was the greatest honour they could offer
him, and putting on his festive robes he willingly
accompanied them.   In spite of her earnest
entreaties his wife was left at liberty.   He was
arraigned before the governor after three months'
imprisonment with four companions, three like
himself members of the Rosary Confraternity, the
fourth, Leonard Chimura, a brother co-adjutor of
the Society of Jesus.   Leonard was the first
questioned, and he answered that he had proclaimed to his countrymen the true faith.   He was
condemned to the flames.   Dominic Georgi, a
Portuguese, was next questioned, and boldly
declared that he had given hospitality to Father
Spinola, S.J., and for this crime had already
suffered more than a year's imprisonment.   John
Xoan   confessed   to   having   lodged   Father
Alphonsus de Mena, and Cosma Taqua, Fathers
John of S. Dominic and Angelo Ferrer.   Then
Andrew   Tocuan   acknowledged   that   Father
Francis de Morales had lived for a long time
in his house, and they were all sentenced to be
burnt alive.   The judge expressed the pain he felt
in seeing Andrew Tocuan in a situation so disgraceful and in being obliged to condemn him to
death.   " You obey your master," was Andrew's
fearless answer ; " I obey mine ; only remember
that outside the Christian Church there is no
salvation."   Before execution he wrote words of
encouragement to his wife and kinsmen, and sent

also a letter to Father Morales, then in prison, of which the following extract is quoted by Meynard :

" I am thankful to you, dearly-beloved Father, because you have been the occasion of my life being given for God. I recommend to you Mary my wife, and Paul my son. When, by the mercy of God, I shall be in heaven, I will pray Jesus, my Master, for your reverence."

On the day of execution the stakes were planted near Nagasaki on a hill surrounded on three sides by the sea. This hill had been already sanctified by the crosses of the twenty-six protomartyrs of Japan. The slope of this hill was covered by an immense multitude, which crowded near the piles of faggots and stretched in dense masses down the hill-sides. Boats were scattered over the sea, and every point commanding a view of the terrible scene was crowded by anxious spectators. Nor were these only prompted by idle curiosity or hatred of the faith, for many among those twenty thousand spectators envied the lot of the five victims who were slowly mounting the hill, which to them was indeed a Calvary. Many were saying their rosary that the grace of constancy might be given to the martyrs. They themselves were rapt in earnest prayer as they walked to the place of torment, and they replied from time to time to the Christians who asked their intercession, bidding them a tender farewell and exhorting them to

stand firm to the last. When arrived at the stakes
they saluted them with words of joy as the instruments of their glory, and turning to each other
they bade adieu until their meeting in paradise.
So loosely were they bound to the stakes that they
might easily have liberated themselves ; but such
was the strength of God's grace in their hearts
that they were not seen to move, or even to writhe
in agony, or to change countenance, when the
flames danced and played around them, and,
leaping up, licked them with their long liquid
tongues. They gazed stedfastly up to heaven.
When the faggots had been kindled, the youths
and maidens of the Confraternity of our Lady,
who filled some boats on the sea, began to chant
psalms in delightful harmony, a foretaste to the
martyrs of the angelic songs. At the same moment
a murmur ran through that immense throng ; the
Christians were invoking the holy Names of Jesus
and Mary. All wept with compassion, mingled
with joy, and exhorted one another to be strong in
the faith. Some even grew so excited that they
were unable to restrain themselves, and would
have rushed into the flames to share the martyrs'
sufferings had they not been reminded that to do
so would be tempting Providence. Amidst such
scenes as these the martyrs went to their Lord :
the flames sank and expired, and the charred
bones which alone remained were broken into
fragments and thrown into the sea. The faithful

however managed to collect some portion of the
holy relics without being able to distinguish to
which of the five they belonged. This martyrdom took place on November 18, 1619.

Andrew Tocuan left behind him Mary his wife,
with a little son, Paul. This woman was well
worthy to be a martyr's wife, and, far from
lamenting her husband's fate as a calamity, she
gloried in it, and earnestly prayed that she herself
might receive a like crown. Three years afterwards this heroic desire was fully gratified, but in
the meantime she had much to suffer owing to the
confiscation of her property, by which she was
reduced to the utmost poverty and became entirely dependent on the charity of others ; but
such afflictions seem trifling to one of her spirit.
Poverty knit more closely the ties that already
united her to the Order of S. Dominic. Long and
ardently had she desired to become a member of
the Third Order, and now that God had deprived
her of her husband and so many of her kindred,
she sought a more numerous family among the
children of S. Dominic. As the immediate cause
of her husband's death had been his generous
hospitality to the friars, the Order was bound to
assist her, and the Father Provincial of the
Philippine islands regarded her as his daughter.
The advantage of the Order was the grand object
of her life, and fervently did she pray in its behalf.
The following letter, addressed to Father John of

S. Hyacinth, shows the fervent spirit of this
Japanese convert :—

"I thank you a thousand times, my Father,
for the large alms you sent me, and still more for
the letter which accompanied it. The holy instructions it contained are, indeed, most necessary in
this time of trial. Most of the fathers of our
Order are in prison and in daily expectation of
martyrdom. The rest are hidden in different
places on account of the persecution. What can
I say of myself ? I have lost all my earthly
possessions, my good husband and my property ;
driven from my house, I am obliged to beg for
food. Living in a little hut, I am supported by
what you send me, and your fathers obtain for me.
But all this is my joy and happiness, especially
when I remember that I am persecuted for having
given shelter to the servants of God—the children
of our father S. Dominic. I would give my life a
thousand times over for any one of them. After
God my only consolation now is to serve them ;
in them I seem to be serving the angels of heaven.
. . . . If it be God's will, I have no other
desire than to suffer martyrdom, and although I
am a great sinner, I trust God will vouchsafe to
give me this grace, through the intercession of
Andrew Tocuan, my husband, and through the
prayers of my fathers of the Order of S. Dominic,
to whom I affectionately commend myself.

Miserable as I am in myself, I feel a strong hope.

" MARY TOCUAN."

In another letter, too long for insertion, she begs for more missionaries to supply the place of those in prison, and announces with great joy that she has been received into the Third Order. Soon afterwards she was left quite alone by the death of her little son Paul, which, she says, happened as a punishment for her sins. Even in her impoverished condition she was a constant benefactress of the Order, and her example and fervent exhortations kept up the courage of the other Christians. Later she glorified God by a martyr's death.

These details are deeply interesting, as showing by the example of one family the saintly spirit which animated the members of the Rosary Confraternity. Many others might be mentioned as proofs of a similar spirit, but their narration would be too lengthy. I must confine myself to a brief mention of those other Rosarians who are enumerated amongst the martyrs beatified by Pius the Ninth. Only nine days after the martyrdom of Andrew Tocuan, the governor condemned eleven Christians to be beheaded on the plea that they were neighbours of those who had harboured the missionaries, and therefore might be supposed to have consented to their crime. Twelve were arraigned before the judge, but, as among the

Apostles, one became an apostate, while the eleven resisted the promises as well as the threats of Gonrocu.   They were all members of the Rosary Confraternity, and were beheaded in the presence of a great crowd on November 29, 1619, on that hill which had already seen so many martyrdoms. The names of these eleven martyrs are given in the list of those beatified under the date of November 29.

Lastly, the triumph of five Japanese Rosarians, who were crucified at Cocura in the kingdom of Bugen, must not be entirely omitted.   The sufferers were Simon Quiota, a man venerable by age and virtue, to whom God had given peculiar power to deliver possessed persons ; Magdalen, his wife ; and their three guests, Thomas Guengoro, Mary, his wife, and James, their youthful son.   Before the governor's tribunal they were stedfast in the faith, and rejoiced when sentenced to be crucified, like S. Peter, with their heads downwards.   The little boy, James, was terribly beaten by the executioners, but nothing could shake his courage, and all five were led to be crucified with their sentence, written in large letters, carried before them, declaring their crime to be an obstinate refusal to abandon the religion of Christ.   Simon and Magdalen remained alive on their crosses till the middle of the next day, and Mary survived somewhat longer.   Thomas, however, and his heroic little son, James, were alive three whole days, and were then despatched by the thrust of a lance.   The virtue and courage of multitudes of Japanese members of the Holy Rosary must be concluded from these few samples. They were an honour to the Order, and true followers of S. Dominic, showing that the Rosary can plant the faith in a new soil as well as destroy a heresy infecting a Catholic people.

CHAPTER VIII.

Father Lewis Florès.

DIFFICULT and dangerous as it was to enter Japan, the members of the different religious orders suffered no opportunity to escape without making the attempt to succour the persecuted Christians. In the year 1620 the Dominicans of Manilla were informed that a Japanese Christian named Joachim Firaiama intended to return to his native country, and some other Japanese Christians were anxious to accompany him. Being a devout man, Joachim was willing to be the means of carrying missionaries to his poor countrymen, though well aware of the imminent risk thus incurred of suffering a cruel death. Accordingly on the day appointed for departure two men came on board in the dress of merchants. To the eye of a stranger there was something remarkable about these two passengers—a calm gravity of deportment and often a look of abstraction that hardly suited their character of merchants, and though dressed with great simplicity and carrying little merchandise, the captain received them with every mark of respect. Frequently they conversed together in a subdued tone, and the sailors sometimes surprised them kneeling in a retired corner of the vessel. Joachim knew these two merchants to be sailing in quest of a pearl of great price—not, indeed, the common red pearls peculiar to Japan, but the souls of its inhabitants, and, if God so willed, the blood-red pearl of martyrdom. Their true names were Father Lewis Florés, of the Order of Friars Preachers, and Father Peter de Zugnica, of the Order of St. Augustine. Father Florés was a Belgian, a native of Antwerp, or, according to another account, of Ghent, where he was brought up, and where his family still remains. He travelled as a merchant into Spain, and afterwards to the West Indies, and feeling a divine call to renounce the world, he became a friar in the Dominican priory of the city of Mexico. There he remained until his sixtieth year, filling the important office of novice-master. Feeling an ever-increasing desire to devote himself to an apostolic life among the infidels, he obtained permission in spite of his advanced years to repair to the Philippines, where for some time he was appointed novice master in the Priory of Manila. Hearing of the opportunity of reaching Japan by the sailing of Joachim's ship, he obtained the desired leave to sacrifice himself for the Christians of that afflicted mission. Ever since his entry into the Order Father Florés had been a model of every religious virtue to his brethren, and his life in the Priory of Manilla seems to reproduce the lives of the Fathers of the Desert. He was a man much given to prayer and mortification, and devoured with zeal for souls and the strictest observation of his rule. His companion, Peter de Zugnica, was a Spaniard, son of a viceroy of Mexico, and at an early age had entered the Order of the Hermits of S..Augustine, in which he was celebrated for holiness of life and skill in preaching. This was his second voyage to Japan.

Joachim's vessel was before long overtaken by one of the tremendous storms common in those seas, and he was obliged to put into Macao for repairs. Setting sail once more, they were between the Chinese coast and the island of Japan, when a Dutch vessel hove in sight. The Dutch were envious of the Spanish commerce with Japan, and being also bitterly hostile to the Catholic faith, they joined with the Japanese in the persecution. Joachim, therefore, concealed the two fathers on the approach of the Dutch vessel, but they were betrayed by one of the Pagan sailors, and out of hatred to them, as supposed Spanish merchants, the ship and everything belonging to it was captured, and taken to the harbour of Firando. The Dutch suspected that the two Spaniards were Missionaries, though they would not acknowledge the fact, and accordingly tortured them most barbarously to extract the truth. They were thrust into a dark and fetid den, fed with rice and water, hung up by a rope with a weight attached to their feet, and Father Florés was bound to a chair, that large quantities of water might be forced down his throat, nearly suffocating him ; but nothing could induce them to acknowledge their character of missionaries. The Christians of Nagasaki were horrified at the news of these barbarities, and several plans were concerted for the rescue of the fathers. Father Didacus Collado, of the Order of S. Dominic, tried to bribe the Dutch sentinel, but this not succeeding, he induced Lewis Yakiki, a Tertiary of S. Dominic, to undertake the dangerous enterprise of rescuing the fathers. His character specially fitted him for this bold adventure. His vigorous and active framè was in keeping with the intrepid courage that filled his heart, and, naturally fond of adventure, when the cause of religion called for an exhibition of bravery and endurance, nothing could daunt the noble spirit of the young Tertiary. The original spirit of the Third Order, when it was a military confraternity, a spirit of chivalry and martial ardour, tempered and directed by supernatural grace, lived again in this Japanese youth. Four other Christians joined him, and having arranged their plans and recommended themselves to God and the prayers of their fellow-Christians, the five young men left Nagasaki, and sailed in a swift boat to the harbour of Firando. They managed to rescue the two fathers, though Florés was almost drowned in entering the boat, and no sooner where they embarked than the five stalwart rowers bent eagerly and silently to their work, and the boat under sail and oars skimmed swiftly over the calm water towards Nagasaki. The Dutch pursued, and soon gained upon them, owing to the rope that secured the sail suddenly breaking. Seeing they were being overtaken, the Christians rowed to land, and tried to effect their escape on foot, but were apprehended by their enemies and carried back to prison. After this bold attempt the Dutch, enraged at so nearly losing their prize, treated the fathers more cruelly than ever, and shortly afterwards Peter de Zugnica acknowledged himself to be a priest. The Dutch were overjoyed at this confession, and immediately delivered him, Joachim, and the Christian sailors to the king of Firando, who imprisoned them on the island of Quinoxima. Father de Zugnica had confessed that he was a missionary, because he found that certain Japanese had recognised him as having been in the empire before in that character. The reason of their persistent silence on this point was the danger to which the avowal would expose Joachim, but this being removed, Father Florés also acknowledged himself a priest and a Dominican, and followed his companion to the prison of Quinoxima.

Gonrocu, the governor of Nagasaki, was at court when the news arrived from the king of Firando that two missionaries had been captured on board a vessel from Manilla, and had been thrown into prison. The emperor, greatly enraged, ordered Gonrocu to return quickly and slaughter the Christians of Firando, Satsuta, and Nagasaki, and he enforced these commands by threatening the governor that if these orders were not faithfully executed he himself should be the first victim. Gonrocu hated the Christians, but it may well be imagined how much that hatred was inflamed by the emperor's menace. At first he used every endeavour to shake the constancy of the captives, especially of the natives, but they despised his fair promises and laughed at his threats, earnestly desiring to suffer for Christ. Two of the sailors who had been released, gave themselves up, protesting that they, too, were Christians, and as guilty as their companions. On August 19, 1622, Gonrocu, seated on his tribunal, sentenced the two religious and Joachim to be burnt alive. The remaining twelve, of whom one was a Tertiary of S. Dominic and the others members of the Holy Rosary, were condemned to be beheaded. The fathers appeared in their religious habits, and accompanied by executioners armed with long iron forks to arrange the faggots, they were led to the sacred hill where so many had already been sacrificed. After their first examination two

Dominican Fathers had obtained access to them and given them the sacraments. Joachim walked along, exhorting the bystanders to forsake the vain service of idols, speaking sometimes what God suggested to his own heart, sometimes acting as interpreter to the missionaries. The guards roughly commanded silence, an order he meekly obeyed ; but afterwards begged to be allowed this last gratification for the few minutes of life that remained. His sweet humility won the permission, and he preached to the people till the procession arrived at the stakes. Seeing that the one prepared for him was badly planted, Joachim secured it himself, and was then loosely fastened to it. The wood of the sacrifice was piled round him and the two priests, but, before the fire was kindled, they had to witness the death of their twelve companions. Opposite the stakes a small enclosure had been raised, and within stood an executioner with drawn sword. One by one the twelve martyrs entered this enclosure, and their heads were immediately struck off. The fires were then kindled, but at some distance from the stakes, so that the martyrs were almost suffocated by the smoke, while the gradually-increasing heat scorched and roasted them. They stood, however, motionless, enduring the torment by the help of earnest prayer for two long hours. Father Peter invoked the glorious S. Augustine, and Father Lewis answered, " Let us persevere ;

S. Augustine is with us." At last death released them, and they received the martyr's palm. Father Lewis Florés fell first, Joachim second, and lastly Father Peter de Zugnica.

For the space of four days and nights the hallowed remains of these martyrs remained exposed, in order that the Dutch, who had denounced them as disobedient to the emperor's decrees, might have the satisfaction of seeing that the supposed crime had been duly punished.

During this time their eyes remained open and fixed on the heavens, which fact, considered as supernatural, is attested in the processes at Manilla. Gonrocu afterwards allowed them to be buried, and a devout widow named Agnes of Corea bought the relics of Father Lewis Florés, and carried them to her house, where Dominican fathers were accustomed to assemble.

After the martyrdom of Father Peter Vasquez, Father Lewis's body was sent to Manilla, and buried in the church of the Friars Preachers. Father Peter Zugnica's relics were deposited in the church of the Jesuit fathers in Macao. The names of these martyrs occur in the list of those recently beatified.

CHAPTER IX.

The Great Martyrdom.

HE martyrdom of Father Florés took place on August 19, 1622. By this time, therefore, Father Thomas of the Holy Ghost, with his companions, Brother Manse of S. Thomas and Paul Nangaoci, had for five years endured the horrors of their prison, and Fathers Angelo Ferrier and Thomas of the Rosary with Brother John Mangoriki had suffered the same tortures for four years. Father Francis de Morales and Father Alphonsus de Mena had been fellow-captives in different prisons for three and a half years; and Fathers Hyacinth Orphanel and Joseph of S. Hyacinth had spent, the first sixteen, the second twelve months in prison. These were now all united in one prison in Omura, constructed especially for their confinement, and with them were many associates of the Holy Rosary, and several members of the Third Order. In the same prison were also nine religious of the Seraphic Order of S. Francis, three fathers and six brothers; and two fathers of the Society of Jesus, with four novices and three catechists. The life these holy confessors led in prison was a standing miracle and worthy of enthusiastic admiration.

More heroic courage was necessary to bear the protracted misery of such a prison than to suffer on the
block or at the stake.   They were all confined
in one chamber, which they were strictly forbidden
to leave under any circumstances.   The stench of
this miserable den was insupportable, and it seems
miraculous its inhabitants could survive.   Their
food was a meagre allowance of rice or badly-
cooked herbs, given them through a hole in the
wall ; their drink was water.   Knives and scissors
were forbidden, so that their hair and beards
became long, shaggy and matted ; lights were
denied them, and even water with which to wash
their garments.   So densely was their narrow
prison crowded that there was scarce room to lie
down ; they were therefore tormented at once by
cold and heat, hunger, thirst, dirt, fatigue, and by
the stifling atmosphere of their prison.   Over all
this patience and Christian endurance reigned
supreme ; no murmur or complaint was heard, so
that the guards were frequently changed, because
they grew compassionate to their victims.

In fact, the prison of Omura was the convent of
a fervent religious community.   The guards, like
those who watched over SS. Paul and Silas at
Philippi, were astonished to hear at midnight the
solemn sounds of a chant in praise of God, for at
that hour the confessors recited Matins, and after
the last notes had been carried away on the night-
air, an hour was give to mental prayer.   Many,

following the example of S. Dominic, offered their blood to God during the darkness of the night under the lash of the discipline. Every evening after Compline the *Salve* was sung to that ancient music so familiar to all the children of S. Dominic, and on Saturday hymns were sung in honour of the mysteries of the Rosary. "The captives," says Father Charlevoix, "added fasts and austerities to their sufferings. A rule was agreed to and faithfully kept. Each day the priests said mass, and were superiors in turn, week by week. The office was recited in two choirs." The means to offer the Holy Sacrifice must have been supplied by the faithful outside, as it is evident, from different accounts, that they contrived to hold some communication with the captives. Extracts are quoted at length by Father Meynard from letters written by the different Dominican priests in prison, which are evidences at once of the heroic virtues of the writers and of the consolations with which God sustained His suffering children. Thus Father Francis Morales thanks God for allowing him to live in that prison, which he styles " most beautiful, and a place dearly to be loved. God is rich and bountiful in His mercy, as I have learnt since my imprisonment, for I did not know before that it was possible a man in this world could feel the excess of joy and gladness that fills my heart. I ask but one thing from God, and that is that I may not depart hence except to die for His Name." Father

Alphonsus de Mena dates his letter, " From my prison, which is the paradise of my delights." Father Angelo Ferrier thus announces his arrest : " Good news! Good news! All is well! I am in prison for Jesus, my love, and I hope to die for Him. Our only fear is lest they may send us to Manilla, and thus prevent us dying for Christ ; but we desire only God's will, and know that we are unworthy to suffer for His holy Name." In fact the only apprehension which at all agitated their minds was the chance that the martyr's crown, now almost within their grasp, should be denied them. But this fear only called forth generous acts of humility and complete abandonment to the will of God. Their feelings may be shortly expressed by that beautifully simple sentence of Father Charles Spinola after describing their sufferings. " In short," he says, "there is much to offer to our Lord." In the midst of their sufferings they were supported by the Holy Communion, which, when the captive priests could not say Mass, Father Dominic Castellet managed sometimes to bring them at the imminent risk of his life.

Gonrocu, in obedience to the emperor's command, had resolved to strike terror into the Christians by mowing down at one stroke the flower of their ranks. On the morning of September 9, therefore, in the year 1622, an officer entered the Satsuta prison with a list of those selected for the next day's combat. Amidst breathless silence he read the names of those who had been condemned, and as each one's name was called he was tightly bound and led outside the prison enclosure. All the priests were included except Father Thomas of the Holy Ghost, and Father Apollinarius Franco, who to their sorrow were omitted, though they had undergone the longest term of imprisonment. The hearts of the chosen band overflowed with joy at the arrival of the long-desired hour, and standing outside their prison they sang psalms of praise to God, thanking Him for the wonderful graces showered upon them during their long confinement, and begging Him to glorify His name by their death. " Either the sword, the fire, or the cross, according to Thy will," was their heroic aspiration, for as yet they were ignorant what death awaited them.

Nagasaki having been chosen as the place of sacrifice, the prisoners were conducted in a large boat to Nangaye, the town in which Alphonsus Navarette had been captured, and as horses were found awaiting their arrival, the whole cavalcade started immediately on their journey. A report had spread that the Christian missionaries from Omura were being conducted to martyrdom, so that the faithful met them while disembarking at Nangaye, and crowding round, demanded their blessing and begged their prayers. A large escort consisting of nearly three hundred soldiers had been sent to accompany the prisoners, who were placed on horseback each with a halter round his neck, one end being held by an armed attendant. The guards were furnished with strong bamboo canes, which enabled them more effectually to keep back the crowd which collected on all sides either from curiosity or devotion. At the head of the procession rode the officer in command, surrounded by twenty lances and an escort of musketeers and bowmen. Night overtook the weary party at a place called Voracam, and here the soldiers hastily enclosed a space of open ground with a palisade, within which the Christian captives spent the night, lying on the bare ground, with nothing to protect them from the pouring rain. Very early in the morning they again mounted on horseback, and the journey was continued, the road being lined with Christians kneeling to receive the last blessing of the martyrs. It must have been difficult for these faithful souls to recognize those they loved so well, and tears of compassion flowed freely when they saw the emaciated forms of the missionaries with their dirty and ragged garments dripping with the night's rain, their hair and beards long and tangled, their cheeks pale with illness, their brows wrinkled and haggard with suffering. They were indeed disguised, transfigured, but with the disguise and transfiguration of Calvary. Salutations and affectionate greetings passed between the prisoners and the faithful, and many were the exhortations on both sides to remain constant to the end.

At last the city of Nagasaki appeared, and the crowd continually thickened. The martyrs were not taken into the city, but were at once conducted to the sacred hill, the holy place of the martyrs. An immense throng of people had already collected on the sides of the hill, which jutting out into the sea, slopes gradually towards the city. Before the arrival of the prisoners bodies of soldiers had been posted in different places to preserve order and to prevent a rescue being attempted. Sixty thousand spectators clustered on the hill, and of these it was computed that thirty thousand were Christians. As the prisoners from Omura first came in sight, a sound of many voices ran through that mixed multitude—exclamations of pity and contempt, recognitions of friends, prayers and aspirations that fortitude might be given the martyrs. Then a deep silence followed. The multitude contemplated the condemned ; the missionaries preached to the dense throng. For a whole hour the martyrs stood on the hill near the twenty-two stakes there planted, waiting for their companions. The priests took this last opportunity of preaching to the people and encouraging the Christians. Amongst the rest Father Francis Morales after declaring that he was about to die for the true Faith begged the faithful not to be scandalized if he manifested any signs of weakness amidst the torturing flames, but to attribute them to the natural shrinking of the flesh, which is weak even when the spirit is willing. Suddenly sounds were

heard from the city ; every eye was turned in that
direction, while cries of "They come! they come !"
were heard amongst the people. Then again followed a general silence, for the strains of voices
singing in harmony filled the air, and a procession
of Christian martyrs issued from the city gate, and
began slowly to ascend the hill. No martyrdom,
even in the early days of the Church, could have
presented a scene more touchingly beautiful. It
was a solemn procession of the Rosary, to end at
the feet of Mary ; a triumphal progress, through the
portal of death, into the kingdom of light. First
came Mary of Fingo, clad in the white habit of the
Tertiaries of S. Dominic, bearing a cross, the stan-
dard of these Christian warriors. Mary, the wife of
Andrew Tocuan, followed, clad also as a Tertiary,
and though only thirty-three years old, her infir-
mities making her unable to walk, she was carried to
martyrdom. Agnes, the wife of the martyr Cosmo
Taquea, and Catherine of Fingo were both Tertiaries, and the latter, says Father Meynard, Prioress
of the Confraternities of the Rosary and the Holy
Name. There were also several members of the
Rosary Confraternity, and some children, one of
them named Peter, only three years old, and carried
in his mother's arms. Another boy of five, also
named Peter, walked alone to martyrdom.

The men formed a second procession. Amongst
them was Rufus Iscimola, Prior of the Rosary,
and Dominic of Chiamgo, who had sheltered a

Dominican father in his house ; Damian with his son (only five years old), and Clement, carrying his infant child of two.*

As the procession moved on, surrounded by guards, the crowd fell back to let the heroes ascend to victory, and even heathen eyes must have moistened with tears to see women of high rank, nurtured in ease and delicacy, carrying their tender infants with them to a public and disgraceful death. What mysterious power must they have acknowledged to be in the Christian religion, to give little children the fortitude to offer themselves willingly to the executioners' sword ! Yesterday Gonrocu had been taught another lesson of Christian heroism. These confessors had stedfastly rejected the fair promises by which he had sought to render them unfaithful to their Lord, and that morning he had condemned them all to be beheaded, a sentence they heard with unfeigned pleasure. During the martyrdom Gonrocu remained within the city, having commissioned an under-official to preside over the terrible scene. This deputy of the governor sat enthroned in state on the dais covered with the finest carpets of China, with a magnificent canopy stretched

* Some difference exists among authors as to the exact number in these two processions, but they agree in all the chief facts. The catalogue at the end, which represents the whole number of martyrs as fifty-two, is the most certain, as it is the list of those beatified. Father Meynard says that twenty-five were burnt and thirty-three beheaded, making the whole number as much as fifty-eight.

above, and surrounded by the great men of Nagasaki.

At last the procession reached the top of the hill, and tender greetings passed between those that composed its ranks and their companions awaiting them at the stakes. Father Francis de Morales saw once more his cherished daughter Mary Tocuan, and this heroic woman, feeble as she was, prostrated herself at his feet, asking his blessing. "Where," said the father, "is your little son Paul?" "He is," said the Christian mother, "where we shall soon be ourselves. God has taken him to paradise."

The priests would not suffer this last opportunity of preaching to the heathen crowd to be lost, and turning to the presiding judge, they declared the truth of Christianity, the folly of idolatry, and protested that, far from coming to Japan on any political errand, according to the assertions of their enemies, they sought only the eternal salvation of souls. The signal was given by the judge, and the twenty-one condemned to the flames were bound loosely to their stakes, so that at any moment they could purchase life by apostasy. Father Boero gives the position occupied by these martyrs from a Japanese picture drawn by an eyewitness. Nearest the sea there were four natives, who had given hospitality to religious, namely, Anthony Sanga, Paul Nagasci, a Dominican Tertiary, Anthony ofCorea, and Lucy, a member of the Third Order of S. Francis. Then

followed the religious from Satsuta—first, Father
Charles Spinola, S.J. ; second, Father Angelo
Ferrer, O.P. ; third, Father Joseph of S. Hyacinth,
O.P. ; fourth, Father Chimura Sebastiano, S.J. ;
fifth, Father Richard, O.S.F. ; sixth, Father
Alphonsus de Mena, O.P. ; seventh, Father Peter
di Avila, O.S.F. ; eighth, Vincent of S. Joseph, lay-
brother, O.S.F. ; ninth, Father Francis de Morales,
O.P.; tenth, Leo, of Satsuma, Tertiary of S. Francis.
After these came five native students of the
Society of Jesus, three Japanese, who deserted
their stakes, as will be seen later, and then another
member of the Society named Brother Luigi
Cavara. To the last stake was bound Brother
Alexis, a professed Dominican novice.

Brother Dominic Mangoriki and Brother Thomas
of the Rosary were among those condemned to be
beheaded, and they all knelt in a line near the
stakes, calmly awaiting the end. The little children
even knelt with quiet gladness, their hands clasped,
their lips moving in prayer, and their eyes looking
upwards to heaven. Father Spinola intoned the
psalm, *Laudate Dominum omnes gentes*, all the
martyrs, and doubtless also the surrounding Christians, taking up the solemn chant of thanksgiving.
*As with one voice they praised and glorified and
blessed God in the furnace* (Dan. iii. 51). An eye-
witness of the scene attested at Manilla that he had
never heard harmony so sweet and joyful, sounding
as if the guardian angels of the martyrs had moved

their tongues. At length the appointed moment
arrived, the signal was given, and in a few minutes
the sword of the executioner, reeking in Christian
blood, had finished its work. Not one of the
martyrs had flinched, each one in turn, meekly bow-
ing to the stroke, had departed to the heavenly
kingdom. The youngest children among them met
their death with the utmost fortitude.

Then the fire was applied simultaneously to all
the stakes, and as soon as the smoke appeared,
curling up in wreaths from the damp wood, a loud
cry was heard on all sides. From the sea, from
every part of the hill, the voice of sympathy and
supplication arose. Thousands joined in it, with
such earnestness that it seemed, says a writer, as if
that vast multitude were about to give up the ghost.
It struck a strange feeling of awe into the judge,
and comforted the martyrs' hearts. It was the
sound of the Christian spectators begging God to
vouchsafe to His servants constancy amid their torments. The wood was damp, the piles extended
some feet from the stakes, and were kindled at such
a distance as to roast and torture the sufferers without causing their deaths. Every moment the
agony increased, as the flames crept nearer and
nearer. If the fire approached some martyr too
rapidly, water was immediately poured upon it, lest
the torture might too speedily be ended. Thus the
first half-hour rolled by, amidst the tears and
prayers of the faithful, the mocking shouts of the

soldiers and the pagan mob, the half-suppressed groans of the martyrs, and their constant cry of " Jesus and Mary."

In the midst of this exhibition of Christian faith a lamentable event took place. Two, or, according to some, three, Japanese were conquered by the violence of their agony. The torment was so terrible that they rushed from their piles, and prostrate before the guards, they implored death by the sword. They would not apostatize, but the agony of the fire they could not endure. Blessed Paul Nangasci, the Dominican Tertiary, was pierced to the heart when he saw their danger, and he left his stake to secure his brethren, and lead them back to the altar of sacrifice. " How is this ? " he cried ; "your sufferings will soon end. In a few moments you will be with the blessed. Take courage, pray for strength, and come with me to die for the love of our Saviour. " Then, setting them an heroic example, he went back over the burning wood, and kneeling at his stake, he embraced it, shedding many tears, and praying with all the force of his soul, he thus remained until released by death. The prayers of this glorious martyr were answered, for those whom the fire had conquered in their turn became conquerors, and, retracing their steps, resigned themselves to their painful death. This is the most consoling account. Father Boero, however, says that these three unhappy men had been, through their own fault, abandoned by God's grace,

owing to some fault committed in prison (Father
Charlevoix adds of disobedience), and that they
apostatized, as Father Spinola had before prophesied
they would, but the judge ordered them, notwith-
standing, to be driven again into the flames.   Boero
doubts if more than two became apostates, and
even these are considered likely to have repented
before their death, but their names are not enrolled
among the beatified.   Bartoli and Charlevoix, by a
strange mistake, reckon Blessed Paul Nagasci among
these, and represent him as an apostate.   Many
proofs of the contrary could be given, but none are
necessary, since Pius the Ninth has solemnly
raised him on the altars of the Church as a glorious
martyr of the Order of S. Dominic.

Before the fire began actually to consume him,
Father Joseph of S. Hyacinth, in imitation of his
Divine Master, cried out, "*I thirst.*" His mouth
was parched, for he had been long exhorting the
Christians with great vehemence to have a tender
devotion to Mary, and to continue faithful in the
practice of reciting the rosary, that it might instruct
them in the Faith after the death of their pastors.
The soldiers mocked his request, but a woman in
the crowd, moved to compassion, managed to give
him a cup of water, with which he refreshed himself
and his companions.   Taking the cup before he
drank, he lifted it high in the air, according to a
Japanese custom, and cheerfully saluted those
around, to the consolation, says an old writer, of

the Christians, and the astonishment of the heathen.

Father Francis de Morales was seen walking amid the flames with most perfect calmness and composure, like one of the three children of Israel in olden days, until at last he fell consumed, and gave his spirit to God. The astonishment of the spectators reached its height when they saw Father Angelo Ferrer rise gradually in kneeling posture several feet above the top of the highest flames. In this marvellous ecstasy he remained for some time in the sight of all. Some hours passed away. At the end of the first Father Spinola went to rest, and one after the other the martyrs died, till few remained to suffer. The throng gradually dispersed, the officials returned to the city, and, as night came on and heavy rain began to fall, the guards alone remained around the smoking ashes. During the whole of that long night Father Hyacinth Orphanel lingered in agony. The wood provided for his pile was green and saturated with water. It smouldered on, bursting occasionally into flames, and even after the morning light had appeared the soldiers heard a faint voice calling on " Jesus and Mary." He suffered for sixteen hours.

The sacred remains were watched by Gonrocu's soldiers for three days and nights without being removed from the place of execution. A native Christian named Leo Fracuzayemon endeavoured to obtain some portion of the relics, but being seized and imprisoned, was himself burnt alive for refusing to abandon his religion.   After three days an immense pile of wood was erected, and the remains of the martyrs, together with sacks full of earth saturated with blood, were thrown upon it.   Any one who approached was beaten, stript, and bound to a stake till the operation was over.   The ashes of this immense pile were carried away to sea, and cast overboard.

Although the heathen did everything to dishonour the relics of the martyrs, God himself was pleased to manifest the glory of His faithful servants by a miraculous light, which shone with great brilliancy over the place of their triumph during the very next night.   Two European fishermen attested on oath that they saw this supernatural light, which remained visible for at least two hours.   It was also deposed on oath in 1630 that, according to a tradition considered authentic by the Christians of Nagasaki, certain Christian fishermen saw during the same night a procession of lights on the sacred hill, headed by one more splendid than the rest.   This was confirmed by the heathen guards, who declared that while they were watching during the night, the mangled and charred remains had suddenly assumed an appearance of perfect integrity and extreme glory, and had formed a procession, singing the praises of the Lord of Heaven.   The first, conspicuous among his fellows for brightness, was said to be Father Spinola, of the Society of Jesus.

Such was the " Great Martyrdom " which will ever render the 10th of September, 1622, a memorable day in the Church. This name it well deserves on account of the number, dignity, and illustrious virtue of the victims, and the atrocious torments many of them endured. All the Orders in Japan shared the triumph, but that of S. Dominic was most numerously represented, losing on that day the finest of its missionaries in Japan. Eight religious, five priests, and three professed brothers, besides numbers of tertiaries and associates of the Rosary, were sacrificed to God in the "Great Martyrdom."

Father Francis de Morales and Alphonsus de Mena were among the first Dominicans that entered Japan in 1601. Many details have already been given of their long mission, so gloriously crowned. It will be interesting to hear a short account of the other religious, though want of space renders it necessary to omit many details recorded by different writers.

Father Angelo Orsucci was an Italian, born in the city of Lucca, May 5, 1573. He received in baptism the name of Michael, which he afterwards changed to Angelo. In his early boyhood he was remarkable for those virtues suited to his years, and was held up as an example to his brothers. His heart was filled with tender love for Mary, which he expressed by daily reciting her Office and the Rosary, and by visiting with great devotion a famous image called " Our Lady of Miracles." He mingled the reading of devout books with his early studies, being especially attracted by accounts of the heroism of the martyrs. While still a youth he received the habit of S. Dominic in the Priory of S. Romanus in his native city, and studied first at the convent of the Quercia in Viterbo, and afterwards in the Minerva in Rome. A story is related of the young Brother Angelo that shows the resolution with which he fought against the inclinations of his nature. Being only fourteen, he found considerable difficulty in rising for midnight Matins, his sleep being at that time so sound. His novice master, to enable him to wake, gave him a cell next to his elder brother, Francis Orsucci, and a rope tied to his foot was passed into his brother's cell. This plan being only partially successful, the fervent novice made a resolution to consider the noise of those who called him to be made by the soldiers who came to crucify Christ. This consideration enabled him to rise at the first sound of the signal, and join with spirit in the praises of God.

After having finished his studies, feeling a great desire to devote himself to a missionary life, he obtained permission to visit Valentia in Spain,

where he enjoyed the privilege of living for some
time in that Priory, made so famous by the sanctity
of its two celebrated sons, S. Vincent Ferrer and
S. Lewis Bertrand. Out of devotion to the first of
these wonderful apostles Father Angelo took the
name of Ferrer, and consecrated himself to a
missionary life under the patronage of S. Vincent.
The first favourable opportunity saw Father
Angelo on his way to the Philippine Islands,
where for many years he laboured with the
utmost zeal on different missions. So much did
he suffer on the mission of New Segovia from his
laborious journeys on foot and other hardships of
the apostolate, that he fell ill, and was obliged to
return to Manilla. For two years he bore a
harrassing sickness with the utmost resignation
and cheerfulness, showing by his virtues that he
deserved his name of Angelo. After his recovery
he was again employed on missions to the natives
of the islands, and then was sent as prior to the
convent in Mexico, especially founded to assist
missionaries on their journey from Spain to the
East. On his return to Manilla his brethren were
about to send him to Rome to represent the
interests of their province, but his humility
prompted him to refuse this office, and beg instead to be despatched on the Japanese mission.
The Father Provincial was long unwilling to
accede to this request, not wishing to part with
so holy a Religious ; therefore, to discover the will

of God the advice of Father Calderon, of the Society of Jesus, was asked. Hearing the circumstances of the case, his decided answer was, "Go by all means, as our Lord will have much glory from it." The provincial, therefore, commanded Father Angelo to depart, and he arrived in Nagasaki on August 12, 1618. To learn the language, he lodged in the house of Cosmo Taquea, a devout member of the Rosary. During the night of December 13 the house was surrounded, and Father Angelo was seized and cast into prison.

Father Joseph of S. Hyacinth, a Spaniard, was professed in the Priory of S. Dominic in the town of Ocãna, a house in which observance was stricter than in almost any convent in Spain. John de Rechac calls it "the chosen dwelling-place of piety." Most of the novices of Castille were sent to Ocãna to be instructed in religious discipline. Father Joseph showed the good fruits of the training he had there received, being remarkable for religious virtue and apostolic zeal. It has already been mentioned that Father Francis Morales sent him to Miako, when the Dominicans were expelled from Satsuma, and that he erected a church there, and afterwards another, dedicated in honour of S. Dominic, at Ozaca, one of the richest and most important towns of the empire. After Father Francis Morales had fallen into the persecutors' power, Father Joseph was elected to succeed him in the office of vicar provincial of the missions, and his heart was afflicted to see the Christians in sad need of spiritual help, while those who longed to assist them were in prison, waiting for death. During his term of office Father Florés was captured, and the vicar provincial tried every expedient to restore him to liberty—with what success has been already seen. On the night of August 17 Father Joseph's time came. He had been hearing a great number of confessions, and was about to retire for some necessary repose, when suddenly his apartments were filled by a multitude of persons, whom he at first took for Christians desiring the sacraments. They were, however, satellites come to apprehend him ; and, with a cord round his neck he was led before the governor, and afterwards imprisoned in Satzuma. He was a singularly eloquent man, and having become very familiar with the Japanese language, he was a most useful preacher. His favourite subject was our Lady of the Rosary, and on this he delivered his last sermon on the day of his martyrdom, his pulpit being the pile on which he was burnt.

Father Hyacinth Orphanel was also a Spaniard, and a native of the kingdom of Aragon. He was professed in Barcelona, and entered the empire of Japan in 1609, when he was about thirty. For eleven years he laboured in different parts of the country. The process of his beatification speaks of charity to the poor as his characteristic virtue, their sufferings temporal as well as spiritual filling his heart with compassion.

When persecution raged with special violence in Arima, he flew to the assistance of the Christians, to comfort them in their trials, and to show them how to suffer for Christ. Father Hyacinth was the author of a history of the Dominican Missions in Japan from the first entrance of the friars until 1620, and the work was continued by Father Collado up to the year 1622. He speaks of himself in this history as "a certain religious of the Order," and under this name mentions some of his labours for the spread of the Christian faith. On one occasion, making a journey into Firando, formerly an Augustinian mission, he was received with the utmost joy, and lodged in the king's palace, thus enjoying full liberty to exercise his apostolic duties among the people. The king was himself an apostate, but at the time of Father Hyacinth's visit was absent, having left the government in the hands of his uncle, a Christian. Another time he travelled about sixty leagues to find a confessor, and at last met a Jesuit father whose sanctity and prudence were of great assistance to his soul. In April of 1621 he was taken, and, after explaining the truth of the Christian faith to the judge, was condemned to the prison of Satsuta. On the way to the prison multitudes of Chris-

tians accompanied him singing the Litanies.
Of the three brothers Dominic, Thomas of the
Rosary, and Alexis, little more is known than that
they were natives who aided the fathers in their
apostolic labours. Brother Dominic, whose secular name was John Mangoriki, and Brother
Thomas of the Rosary received the habit, or at
least made their profession, in the prison of Satsuta, having proved themselves well worthy of
that honour. Brother Thomas is mentioned by
Father Meynard as a priest, but in the processes
he is spoken of as a professed choir brother.
Alexis * was burnt, Dominic and Thomas beheaded, because sufficient stakes were not provided. Thomas of the Rosary being young and
handsome, the judge offered to spare his life if he
would deny that he knew the fathers of S.
Dominic, but he answered with vehemence :
" How could I say that without offending God by
a lie ? I both know these religious, and for years
I have endeavoured to assist them in their work
for the conversion of souls."

The great martyrdom did not satisfy Gonrocu's
thirst for blood, and on the very next day " he beheaded, at Nagasaki, Gaspard Cotenda and eleven
others, all of the Third Order." † Cotenda was a

* It seems doubtful whether Alexis was, strictly speaking,
a religious. Father Collado says he received the habit
from devotion to the Order just before his martyrdom.

† Father Meynard, *Missions dans l'extrême Orient*,
vol. i. p. 317.

kinsman of the king of Firando, and a catechist of the fathers of the Society of Jesus.

Father Thomas of the Holy Ghost was still in prison, although he had been captured the earliest of all the Fathers, while completing Alphonsus Navarette's work. Great was his grief when his companions preceded him to martyrdom, but he found comfort in the divine will, humbled himself profoundly, and acknowledged himself un-worthy of the martyr's crown. It was not, however, long delayed. On September 12 (only two days after the great martyrdom) his weary imprisonment ended, and he was burnt with his companions, Brother Mance of S. Thomas and Brother Dominic of Fiunga, professed brothers of the Order. Father Apollinarius Franco and two native Franciscan novices suffered on the same day. Father Thomas was a Spaniard, whose family name was Zumarraga, and was a native of Vittoria. He made his profession as a religi-ous of S. Dominic in the Priory of S. Stephen in Salamanca on January 19, 1594. Studying in the Priory of S. Gregory at Valladolid, he remembered "that wisdom will not enter into a malicious soul, nor dwell in a body subject to sin," and there-fore moulded his life after the example of the saints of his Order. His spirit of observance was most rigid. In 1601 he started for the eastern missions, and on his journey to the sea-port he travelled on foot, in imitation of our

Holy Founder, without any provision for the journey. In 1602 he arrived in Japan, and during the next year was sent back by Father Francis Morales to give an account in Manilla of the success of the first missions. On this voyage the ship caught fire, and when death appeared to stare every one in the face, Father Thomas cast his rosary and some relics into the flames, and they were immediately extinguished. He returned to Japan in 1604, and for some time held the office of vicar provincial, in which he was succeeded by Alphonsus Navarette. He laboured until 1617 in various parts of the empire, spending some time in Miako, and working without intermission for the good of souls. His patience in prison has been frequently mentioned. The two choir brothers were catechists to the fathers and were youths of eminent virtue, imitating the example they saw in the fathers of the Order. It is to be regretted that so few details are known of the lives of these native Religious, who met their death for the Faith with a heroism quite equal to the missionaries from Europe. Brother Mance of S. Thomas was a professed choir religious, and had been of great assistance to Father Thomas of the Holy Ghost. It is doubtful whether Brother Dominic belonged to the First or Third Order. The processes of Manilla state that he received the habit in prison, while some writers represent him as a choir

religious, and others as a lay brother.   Father
Collado mentions a secular imprisoned with Father
Hyacinth Orphanel, from whom he received the
habit before his death.   This is probably the
same Brother Dominic.   Their triumph may
almost be reckoned part of the great martyrdom.

The cruel Suchendaiu, who had presided on
September 10, was speedily overtaken by the
justice of God.   When sitting at table, this
miserable man suddenly fell, struck by an invisible
hand, and when his attendants raised his corpse,
they found it scorched as though it had been
roasted over a slow fire.

———

CHAPTER X.

Martyrdom of Brother Lewis Yakiki.—Father
Didacus Collado.—Life and Martyrdom of
Blessed Father Peter Vasquez.

THE brave and generous young tertiary,
Lewis Yakiki, had been in prison since
the failure of his plan for the rescue of Father
Florés.   A crime so great in the eyes of the
governor called for no ordinary punishment, and
he was determined to shake the faith of this noble
Christian, or else to make him a terrible example
of the folly of resisting the emperor's commands.
Lewis was accordingly thrown into prison, with

his wife, his two children, and the four companions of his bold adventure. The horrible barbarity of the torments inflicted upon him made his sufferings more grievous, and his triumph more glorious, than almost any previous martyr in Japan. Christian modesty forbids a full description of the atrocious tortures he endured, but, for his honour, and that of the Order of which he was so distinguished an ornament, they must not be entirely passed over. Before he received his eternal crown at the stake, he was subjected to seventeen different kinds of torture, each more terrible than the preceding. A description of some of these will serve as specimens of what many other martyrs afterwards endured. First he was tortured by the trial of water. This consisted in pouring a very large quantity of water down the sufferer's throat, and then forcing him to disgorge it by means of extreme pressure with a board upon the stomach. During this hideous operation the blood often flowed from the martyr's mouth, ears, and nostrils. His right hand alone was free, in order that he might give the signal of apostasy. Sometimes this torment was inflicted several times in succession. Unable thus to shake Lewis's constancy, the judge ordered his flesh to be torn with red-hot pincers and instruments like the claws of birds, and when his whole frame was so dreadfully lacerated that " from the sole of his foot to

I

the top of his head no sound place appeared," his tormentors cut open his shoulders and poured molten lead into the gaping wounds. Their next contrivance was to pierce his legs and thighs, introducing into them long rushes, which they worked backwards and forwards, as though they intended to saw the flesh from the bones. Lastly, they thrust sharp-pointed sticks deep into his body, avoiding any vital organ, and then they roughly snatched out these skewers, causing the martyr inconceivable anguish. During these and many other torments the truly heroic courage of Lewis remained unshaken, and the only cry the persecutors could wrest from him was the Names of "Jesus" and "Mary." After thus exhausting every invention of the most refined cruelty on his body, the inhuman governor of Omura tried to overcome him by punishing those he loved more than himself. His beloved wife and his two children—Andrew, only eight, and Francis, only four years old—were led to the place of execution, and Lewis had to choose between denying the faith and seeing his family slaughtered. Without a moment's hesitation the saintly martyr seized the tender Francis and presented him to the executioner. He loved his family too well to deprive them of an eternal crown.

Nothing remained but to condemn him to the flames. As his whole body was one ghastly wound, the executioners desired to carry him to the stake in a palanquin, but he refused this indulgence, saying, with noble courage, " Jesus Christ, for whom I have suffered, will give me strength to walk on foot," and, setting forth with a cheerful countenance, he was able, to every one's astonishment, to walk the whole way, proclaiming with a loud voice the truth of Christianity. The still bleeding heads of his wife and children were placed before the stake, but his martyr's heart rejoiced that his beloved ones were in Paradise. Amidst the flames he refreshed and strengthened himself by invoking aloud the holy Names of Jesus and Mary, while the Christian spectators echoed back these sacred Names, joining their prayers with the dying martyr's. This so enraged the pagan soldiers that they employed heavy blows to enforce silence, and one Christian bystander was struck dead, his head cloven asunder, while the holy Names were on his lips. After suffering for an hour and a half, this true son of S. Dominic went to join his brethren in glory. Those who had been his companions in the attempted rescue of Father Florés were beheaded, but are not among the number of the beatified.

Fierce as the persecution was, it is remarkable that the native Christians were unmolested, unless they entertained missionaries at their houses, concealed them from the authorities, or contrived to introduce them into the empire. These actions were considered in Japan by the emperor, as they were considered in England by Elizabeth, in the light of high treason against the state. In both countries they were punished with the most barbarous severity. In both the object of the penal laws was the same—the extirpation of the Catholic faith. To persecute each individual Christian would have been to decimate the people, to depopulate towns and even districts, so that the emperor determined to destroy the flock by murdering the faithful shepherds. Christians were allowed to pray aloud around the stake at which a martyr was burning, and publicly to ask his blessing, but if a missionary was discovered in their houses, not only they and their family were slaughtered, but often their unconscious neighbours were involved in the same ruin.

With such severity had the laws been enforced that in 1622, after the martyrdom of Father Thomas of the Holy Ghost, only three Dominican priests remained in Japan. Their names were Didacus Collado, Dominic Castellet, and Peter Vasquez.

Of these, Father Collado alone lacked the martyr's crown, but not through cowardice or want of zeal. Though certain authors have written vehemently against him, charging him with cowardice and envy, it seems beyond all question that he was a good religious and a most zealous missionary. I shall not enter into the controversy concerning him, which would be as little interesting as profitable to the reader, but shall content myself with quoting some passages from Father Meynard's book, in which he describes his character :—

"This year (1619) one of the most zealous and most illustrious children of St. Dominic, the indefatigable Didacus Collado, arrived in Japan. This man of God, powerful in good works, and gifted with wonderful energy of character, came to take part in the conflict at a most critical and solemn moment. The prisons of Omura were crammed with captives ; priests, religious, cate-chists, and the faithful of all classes had been thrown together into chains. The Church stood in sore need of a leading spirit, bold in action " (vol. i. p. 288).

In another place in the same volume Father Meynard adds : "Didacus Collado was, with-out question, a holy religious and an untir-ing missionary, in spite of the reproaches which his zeal has sometimes brought upon him. Though frequently condemned to death, and constantly pursued by the Japanese authorities, he persevered in his apostolic work, baptising, hearing confessions, visiting the Chris-tian prisoners, assisting the martyrs, and carrying away their relics. The business of the missions obliged him to go to Rome, where he dwelt for some years, says Father Fontana, who was himself in Rome at the time, with the reputation of being a truly apostolic man, most zealous for the conversion of the heathen. In 1634 he again started from Spain with twenty-three missionaries, and died four days afterwards, a victim of his zeal in hearing confessions on a shipwrecked vessel " (vol. i. p. 321).

Father Collado presided over the missions in the character of vicar provincial after the capture of Father Hyacinth, and continued the history of the missions down to the end of 1622, including the "Great Martyrdom," of which he was an eye-witness.

On S. Mary Magdalen's day, in the year 1621, Father Peter Vasquez, or, as he is often called, Peter of S. Catherine, arrived in Japan to assist his brethren. He was a Spaniard, born in the town of Berin in Galicia, and in his eighteenth year took S. Dominic's habit at Madrid, studying after his profession at Segovia and Avila. The priory in which he passed his noviciate was dedicated in honour of Mary, and " Father Peter placed himself entirely in her hands, keeping the eyes of his soul ever fixed upon her, as the eyes of a handmaid are directed to her mistress." *
Even during the period of his studies he devoted much time to prayer, and was considered a model

* *Historia de la Provincia de S. Rosario*, vol. i. p. 540.

of religious virtue. The modesty of his exterior was the sign of his interior recollection, and the few words he spoke were generally about heavenly things, of which alone he cared to converse. Feeling a desire to spend himself for his neighbour in the missionary life, he implored light from heaven to guide his decision. The result is thus announced by Father Advarte :— "In the year 1613, when I was, for the second time, going round the priories of Spain in search of subjects, Father Peter offered himself to me in the priory of S. Thomas in Avila, and I gratefully accepted him." During the long and tedious journey he behaved as if in a priory of the strictest observance, travelling on foot from the seaport to Mexico, and then to Acapulco, and after his arrival he laboured among the natives, particularly in the mission of New Segovia, with the utmost devotedness. The intelligence of the martyrdom of Blessed Alphonsus Navarette excited a holy emulation in his heart, and he entreated permission to go and share the glories of the suffering Church in Japan. For two years before starting he earnestly recommended his design to God, redoubling his prayers, disciplines, and fasts to move the Divine Majesty to bring his cherished hopes to a happy issue. In spite of the vigorous measures taken by the authorities to prevent missionaries entering the empire, he was able to land at Nagasaki with Father

Dominic Castellet, both disguised in secular costume. This was on July 22, 1621, (about a year before the martyrdom of Father Flores,) and the very day he arrived six Christians were beheaded, and shortly afterwards the vicar provincial, Father Joseph of S. Hyacinth, was captured. This proved to Father Peter that his own time was short, and urged him to walk while he had the light. After staying three months in Nagasaki he settled in a small village in the vicinity to perfect himself in the language, and at Pentecost of the year 1622 he returned to the city. Before August he had heard three thousand confessions. In a letter quoted by Father Advarte he describes how he ventured in disguise into the prisons where the Christians were confined, and gave them the holy sacraments. He passed by eight sentinels without being discovered, in the disguise of a Japanese guard or jailor, with two large swords slung at his side. Interesting details are also given in this letter of his labours, and those of Didacus Collado and Dominic Castellet, among the Christians whose confessions they managed to hear during the darkness of the night. On the day of the Great Martyrdom he once more penetrated into the prisons and administered the sacraments to those about to suffer. Every effort was made to apprehend him, for two apostates whose confessions he had heard in prison had reported to the governor that a Dominican of the name of "Enchizayemon Peter" had visited the captives in prison. This was the name Father Peter had assumed, the Japanese always placing the family name first. In spite of these traitors he escaped detection. Father Dominic Castellet, in a letter to the provincial of the Philippine Islands, speaks in the highest terms of Father Peter, and, amongst the rest, he says :—"Father Peter was sent on an expedition into the kingdom of Arima, where he remained two months, encouraging the Christians and hearing their confessions. This ministry was most successful, for in that short time he heard more than a thousand confessions, and reconciled many apostates. On his return to Nagasaki he renewed his labours with his accustomed generous self-denial. He preferred attending the poor to the rich, saying that the rich could more easily obtain help and advice, whereas the poor were often forsaken. He would never visit any house except to perform some duty of his ministry, saying that, had he desired a pleasant life, he would never have devoted himself to the apostolic work, but, having done so, he cared for nothing else. Lest any might suffer on his account, he changed his lodgings almost every day, and allowed nothing but extreme illness to interrupt his constant labour. Thus, during the seventeen months he was at liberty, he administered the sacrament of penance to above seven thousand persons, spending sleepless nights in the exercise of his ministry." This letter enables us to understand the advice which some of his friends, guided by worldly prudence, gave Father Peter:—"Be moderate," they said; "abate your ardour, and live in seclusion, awaiting more help from Manilla." "No," replied the apostle, "now is the moment to prove ourselves true children of S. Dominic, inheriting his spirit; and to show that, if some shepherds hide themselves through fear of the wolves, the 'Dog of S. Dominic' continues to bark and to expose itself without fear." It is wonderful that Father Peter could have remained so long actively engaged in Nagasaki without being apprehended. He seems to have considered this almost miraculous, for he writes:—"I am not yet taken; but not from lack of danger. I have not been discovered because still unworthy to suffer death for Jesus Christ. I take neither more nor less precaution than formerly, and often pass close by those in search of me." During the Easter season the authorities were more than usually vigilant, knowing that to be a time of special solemnity among the Christians. During Holy Week Father Peter remained in Nagasaki, administering the sacraments undiscovered, but this was the closing scene of his apostolic career.

Father Dominic Castellet had discovered in the

mountains near Nagasaki a secret hiding-place, which Father Peter considered a suitable spot to deposit a most precious treasure, hitherto in the keeping of Agnes of Corea, a fervent Christian woman of the city and a great benefactress of the Order. This treasure was the hallowed remains of the martyr, Blessed Lewis Florés. Before setting out on a second journey into the kingdom of Arima, Father Peter made all the necessary arrangements for the removal of the holy relics. The place was surrounded by rocks covered with brambles, and between them spaces grown over with stout tall rushes. All around was a complete desert. The relics were secretly transported to this hiding-place, and the fathers and some native Christians were joyfully venerating them, when a slight rustle among the reeds startled Father Peter. Looking in the direction of the suspicious sound, he saw the satellites of the governor of Nagasaki watching the little assembly of the faithful. He felt that his hour was come, but without losing his presence of mind he signalled to his companions to fly with the relics, while he also strove to escape. Father Dominic Castellet, being well acquainted with the place, easily baffled his pursuers; but Father Peter, unable to force his way through the thick reeds, " was captured like a bird in the snare of a fowler." * He afterwards

* John de Rechac.

wrote the following letter to Father Dominic, giving an account of his capture:

"My dear Brother,

"When you made that turn which secured your escape, I tried to follow your steps, but our Lord stopped me, it being His will that I should pay the price of the sins and negligences I have been guilty of while working in His vineyard, and particularly of the bad example my lukewarmness has been to the Japanese Christians. God allowed me to become entangled in a thicket, and two soldiers casting themselves upon me, threw a rope around my neck, and then bound the same rope so tightly round my wrists that the blood burst forth, causing me the utmost pain. Next they secured me to a stake while continuing their search for you, but, not finding you, they at last led me away captive. We travelled by land, the soldiers delighted at their prize, and I still more overjoyed in being judged worthy to suffer for Christ. I was much encouraged by noticing that we entered Nagasaki by the street of S. John. I was at once conducted to the governor's tribunal, a large crowd of the faithful following and rending the air with their cries of grief. Their sorrow weighed heavily upon my heart."

At the tribunal he boldly confessed his faith, and was ordered to prison till the appointed time for his execution. The prison was already full, and the result is thus related by Father Peter himself in the letter already quoted : " On my arrival at the prison a great joy awaited me. In order to make room for me, they were obliged to release a robber. I thought of Barabbas." Besides this another point of resemblance to his Divine Master was noticed in Father Peter. He suffered at the age of thirty-three.

In this prison he remained till the feast of Corpus Christi, and was then removed to Omura. On the way the faithful crowded round to ask his blessing, in spite of the rattans of the soldiers, and Dominic Castellet met him in disguise, kissed the martyr's hand, and bathed it with his tears. Father Peter prophesied that assistance would soon be sent him. The lamentations of the people as the ship sailed for Omura were echoed from the hills, " as if," says John de Rechac, " the very rocks were moved to compassion."

In Omura his imprisonment was terrible. The miserable cage in which he was confined, exposed alike to heat or cold, was between six and seven feet high and the same in width, while its length was only two or three feet more. Within these narrow limits four were confined besides Father Peter, namely, Father Lewis Sotelo, Lewis Lapandra, and Brother Lewis Baba (Franciscans), and Father Michael Carvailho, of the Society of Jesus. These confessors were left to languish in prison for above fourteen months, and considering the size of their cage, it seems miraculous that they survived. The only earthly comfort these suffering Christians possessed was the service rendered them by a little Japanese girl of seven. She brought them water, writing materials and other things, which she skilfully hid from the guards. Earnest and constant prayer was their stay and support, together with the strong tie of supernatural charity that united them. It is needless to explain that crowded thus together they must have caused many involuntary sufferings to each other, but nothing broke the harmony of their self-denying love. Spaniard, Japanese, and Portuguese, forgetful of national differences, lived like brothers, with one heart and one soul. They proved the divinity of their religion by this heroic charity, according to that test given by our Lord :—" By this shall all men know you are My disciples, that you have love one for another."

Worn out with the fatigues of his apostolic labours, Father Peter was twice during the time of his imprisonment at the point of death. The first time his companions asked for some medical aid which was refused, but earnest prayer obtained some renewal of strength for the sufferer. The second time the guards represented that unless sentence were immediately passed Father Peter would die in prison, and Gonrocu, unwilling to suffer his prey to escape, ordered the captives to be burnt alive. Exclamations of joy burst from their lips when they heard this sentence, and the good news so much revived Father Peter, who was in his last agony, that he was able to rise and walk to the place of execution, which was on a plain about three miles from Omura.

Before the fires were kindled, the rope that bound Father Peter became unfastened, and the executioner mounted roughly on his shoulders to secure it, an insult which the holy man endured with unruffled patience, though it caused him much suffering. Brother Lewis Baba, when the fire had consumed the rope that bound him, prostrated himself, half-burnt as he was, before each of the priests to ask their blessing. Three hours after they were all with God. The 25th of August was that year a Sunday and the feast of S. Lewis of France, and by a singular coincidence three out of the five martyrs were named Lewis. All the five were beatified by Pius the Ninth.

The ashes of these martyrs, whose dead bodies were re-burnt, to prevent them being carried away by the Christians, were cast into the sea. Father Dominic Castellet, however, managed to secure a small portion of the relics of Blessed Peter Vasquez.

CHAPTER XI.

Life and Martyrdom of Blessed Lewis Bertrand. —The Fires of Mount Ungen.—Blessed Father Dominic Castellet—his Labours and Martyrdom.

ATHER PETER'S prophecy to Dominic Castellet was fulfilled before his martyrdom by the arrival of three Dominican priests. —Fathers Dominic Erquicia, Luke of the Holy Ghost, and Lewis Bertrand.

It was a generous sacrifice on the part of the Fathers of Manilla to part with these men, the flower of their province. Father Dominic was a man of remarkable ability and considered the best preacher in Manilla. Father Luke was professor of philosophy in the convent of S. Thomas in Manilla. The voyage was full of disasters, placing at times the lives of all on board in danger, but the worst misfortune was the loss of one of their companions, Father Didacus Ribera, who sank under the effects of an accidental explosion of a loaded gun which lodged two bullets in his thigh. No surgical aid being at hand, he expired after twenty-four hours of acute suffering, borne, writes Father Dominic, with a patience and submission to the Divine Will which was our only comfort. Father Didacus was a man of considerable reputation for learning, and was employed in teaching theology when assigned by his superiors to the Japanese Mission. After a narrow escape from being captured by pirates, the missionaries at last arrived in Nagasaki, where they landed by night in the disguise of native merchants.

The Blessed Father Lewis Bertrand had the distinguished honour of belonging to the family of the illustrious Saint and Apostle of the West Indies, who nearly a century before had dis-played, to both the Old and the New World, such a marvellous example of sanctity. What higher praise can be given to Father Lewis than to say that he was not content to bear the same name, but that he earnestly endeavoured to imi-tate the religious virtues and apostolic labours of the glorious S. Lewis Bertrand? He was born in the city of Barcelona, and was called Lewis after his illustrious ancestor. The name of his family was Exarch, which shows that he was a kinsman of the Saint on the female side, that being the name of the saint's mother. In him was exemplified that saying of Holy Writ, " Blessed is the man that has borne the yoke from his youth," for in imitation of his patron he entered the Order of S. Dominic, in the strict

K

Priory of S. Catherine the Martyr, in his native
city, while only fourteen years old, obeying, at
this early age, the call of God to forsake the
world and his father's house with the simplicity
of the young prophet Samuel. Though he had
abandoned the dangers of the world while his
innocence was still unsullied, he treated himself
during his noviciate as the worst of sinners. His
master had frequently to restrain the ardent
desire the youthful novice showed for every
kind of mortification, and to take from him the
disciplines and other instruments of penance with
which he mortified his tender body. Fasting,
watching, and prayer were his delight, and the
Fathers of the Priory were astonished at the
mature grace and virtue displayed by the young
Religious. S. Lewis Bertrand lived again in the
person of his kinsman. After his profession the
diligence with which he studied in no way dis-
tracted his mind from God, for without encroach-
ing on the time devoted to study, he spent all
his leisure in earnest prayer, nourishing the flame
of love in his heart, together with the light of
truth in his intellect.

Having thus imitated S. Lewis in his student's
life, he felt drawn by the Holy Ghost to
follow him also into foreign lands for the
benefit of souls, lost in the darkness of
heathenism. Hearing of the regular life and
apostolic zeal of the religious of the Province

of the Holy Rosary, he entreated his superiors to send him there, and, grieved as they were to be deprived of such a model of religious perfection, they recognised the will of God and granted his petition. He arrived at the Priory of Manilla in the year 1618, and though not yet ordained Priest, he was ordered at once to study the language of the natives, that he might be employed in their instruction. He soon became sufficiently familiar with this language, and also with Chinese, so that after his ordination he laboured with great success among the Indians and Chinese settlers. In 1622 the news of the Great Martyrdom raised a universal desire among the members of the Philippine Province to win a like crown, and to walk in the footsteps of their brethren. All could not be spared, but Lewis Bertrand was one of the happy few selected. He immediately applied himself to the study of the language, and on July 19 in the year following he effected an entrance into Japan. Though the "Benjamin" of the Province, as Father Advarte calls him, he had been chosen on account of his distinguished sanctity and talent.

At that time the chief seat of persecution was the city of Nagasaki, owing to the extreme hatred entertained against the Christians by the two under-governors, one of whom was an apostate. Many of the faithful had taken refuge in other kingdoms. On his arrival, therefore, the

Vicar Provincial assigned Omura to Father Lewis
as his mission, and owing to the small number
of religious he was obliged to depart alone.
His apostolate lasted only three years, during
which time he wrought wonders, converting the
heathen, confirming the faith of the Christians,
spending whole nights in hearing confessions, and
esteeming every labour easy and every suffering
sweet, if there was a hope of leading one soul
to Christ.

The poor Christians of Omura looked on
Father Lewis as an angel sent from heaven for
their welfare. Dressed as a Japanese peasant,
barefoot, or shod only with sandals, he journeyed
through the province, regardless of the cold of
winter or the heat of summer, both of which in
Japan are extreme. " We rejoice," said one of
his companions, " when the weather is bad, for
then we are less likely to be watched."

Father Lewis selected the cabin of a poor
woman, named Martha, a leper, for his lodging,
both because thus he was more hidden, and
because she was neglected and despised by the
world. Two of those curious crosses occasionally
found during the persecution in the heart of a
forest-tree were discovered about this time, and
one being given to Father Lewis, the other to
Father Francis of Mary, a Franciscan, they
inspired both these holy men with a fresh hope
of martyrdom, which was soon realised. Father

Lewis gives an account of his capture in a letter
to Father Anthony of the Rosary, the adminis-
trator of the diocese of Macao, in which he
humbly thanks God for allowing him to suffer
for His Name, and makes a solemn offering of
his life to his Lord. A traitor discovered the
place of his concealment, which was suddenly
surrounded by soldiers sent to arrest the servant
of God, with his two companions, the one an
old man who for a long time had acted as
guide to the missionaries, the other a youthful
catechist. Seeing that his hostess was a helpless
old leper, the guards left her unmolested, and it
was only at her earnest entreaty that she also
was carried to prison. "The first night of my
captivity," says the martyr, "I was not bound
with these chains, which are so sweet to bear,
but I was closely bound by the chains of Divine
Love."

About a year was spent by these martyrs in
prison, during which time the persecution raged
in every part, and many received the crown of
martyrdom. Shortly before their execution, the
two Japanese taken with Father Lewis made
their professions as lay-brothers of the Order,
one taking the name of Mance of the Cross, to
commemorate the finding of the miraculous cross
above mentioned, the other, Peter of S. Mary.
The old leper, Martha, became a member of the
Third Order. Father Lewis was able to offer the

Holy Sacrifice, after which the vows were pronounced with great fervour. On July 26, 1627, they all glorified God in the flames.

The Christians managed to secure the head of the Blessed Father Lewis Bertrand, and this precious relic was afterwards taken to Spain, where, during the year 1765, God was pleased to honour it with a remarkable miracle. Father Pius Vives was commissioned to carry the relic through Spain, to consign it to the Priory of S. Dominic in Barcelona. Being in weak health, it was dangerous for him to be exposed to bad weather, but he was several times obliged to travel on foot during storms of rain, while passing through Catalonia. After the journey he deposed on oath that during the whole time he was carrying Father Lewis Bertrand's head, he was never touched by a drop of the rain that poured around him. His companion, Father Baptist Salva, testified to the truth of this assertion.

The number of victims put to death about this time by torments of the most hideous description, passes all computation. The names of most of these Christian heroes are unknown to man, though their glory will be revealed at the judgment day. Some grew faint-hearted under the terrible ordeal, and consented to deny their faith, but these renegades were few compared to the immense number of the faithful and valiant soldiers of the Cross. But there was one torture suggested by the diabolical ingenuity of the persecutors which must not be passed over without more particular mention. Whoever has read any account of the Christians in Japan, must have a vision of the fires of Mount Ungen indelibly fixed in his memory. The very sight of that terrible volcano must have made the bravest tremble. Scorched and desolate rise the sides of this mountain towards the craters which form its summit, and which are separated from one another by calcined rocks and crags of fantastic shapes. It seems a spot that has fallen under the special curse of God, and its chief crater, looking like an ebullition from the lake beneath, "that burneth with brimstone and fire," has received the fitting title of "the mouth of hell." This chasm is filled with a boiling sulphurous liquid, emitting a suffocating stench, one drop of which, touching the human frame, causes intense suffering. To this scene of woful desolation the poor Christians were dragged, and then, horrible to relate, were slowly dipped into the sulphurous abyss, and drawn up before life was extinct, only to be again lowered into the burning gulf when their strength was partially restored. Others were stretched upon the barren rocks, and drop by drop the liquid fire was poured upon their naked bodies, eating away the flesh and penetrating even to the bones, until the whole became one writhing mass of gangrened flesh. Some martyrs were tortured in this manner for five days in succession, and then abandoned to linger in agony, till released by death. Amongst the multitudes of Christian warriors who thus, and in other ways, gained the crown of martyrdom, many were Rosarians and Tertiaries of S. Dominic, but the details of their triumphs are unknown. The scene of this atrocious barbarity has now assumed a different aspect, and a more humane use. The Japanese have discovered that, properly diluted, this sulphurous liquid possesses considerable medicinal virtue, and accordingly, says a recent missionary, "they have changed the barren region that surrounds those frightful abysses into a place for baths and pleasure-houses." *

During these efforts of the demon to destroy the Church in Japan, the zeal and courage of the apostolic missionaries of the different Orders seemed rather to increase. When the persecution was at its height, Father Dominic Castellet performed wonders of missionary labour, traversing during the space of seven years the provinces of Omura, Arima, Firando, and Nagasaki, everywhere converting the heathen and evangelising the Christians. After the capture of Father Peter, as related in the last chapter, Father Dominic was for some time the only Dominican priest in Nagasaki, Omura, and the adjacent country. He was born in Catalonia in the year 1592, and

* *Annals of the Propagation of the Faith*, March, 1868.

took the habit of S. Dominic in the Priory of Barcelona in the year 1608, adopting at his profession the name of our holy Father himself. In his noviciate, and more especially after his ordination, he proved himself a religious of great virtue, and loved labour for souls as much as ordinary men love repose. In 1613 the illustrious Father Advarte, afterwards Bishop of the Philippine Islands, was travelling in Spain in search of subjects for that distant province, and one of the first to offer himself was Father Dominic Castellet. The prospect of dangers by sea and land and the certainty of a life of hardship and suffering only increased the ardour of the young priest.

On his way through Mexico he was delayed for the space of two years in the Priory of S. Hyacinth, where he gave constant proof of his charity, humility and love of prayer. Besides the two hours' meditation made in community, he devoted much time to prayer, and his delight was to serve his brethren, sweeping out the cells, making the beds, and helping in the kitchen. In 1615 he arrived in Manilla. For seven years he preached in the Philippine Islands, and at the end of that period had the satisfaction of being sent to Japan. At the time when the search for missionaries was the strictest, he escaped detection for seven years, though constantly employed in active work for souls. We are told

that he scarcely ever lay down to repose his weary
body.   The nights were constantly spent in
harassing journeys, barefoot, through snow or
over sheets of ice, or along miry and rocky paths.
Nor did this satisfy his zeal, for during all these
astounding labours he was an exact observer
of his austere rule, and kept the fasts and
abstinences as strictly as when within his convent
walls.   This generosity and faithfulness no doubt
sustained him in his toil, and obtained grace to
enable him to do so much in God's service.

At last the end befitting such a life drew near,
and Father Dominic was imprisoned at Nagasaki.
Here, to his joy, he found himself among his
brethren, for, besides many other Christians, two
lay-brothers and about twenty-three professed
Tertiaries of the Order welcomed him as their
fellow-captive for Christ.   The presence of the
saintly Dominican was not merely an extreme
pleasure to those confessors of the faith, but a
solid spiritual blessing.   He drew up a rule of
life, which all followed.   "At midnight," says
Father Meynard, "the prisoners rose and prayed
for an hour.   At four o'clock they again rose and
made their meditation till six, when Father
Dominic offered the holy Sacrifice, and his
companions received Communion, the rest of
the morning being spent in private devotions.
Their scanty allowance of food was given them
at mid-day, and at three o'clock they recited

Vespers and Complin, with the Litany of our Lady, followed by mental prayer till half-past five. Matins were then recited, the darkness making it impossible to say the office at midnight; the remaining part of the evening was spent in spiritual conferences, examination of conscience, and singing hymns. Many every day disciplined themselves with great severity." In fervent piety and strict religious observance such as this the days of their captivity passed by, and the joy which filled Father Dominic's heart at last overflowed, and he exclaimed—"Now I am a Christian! Now, at last, I can glory in being a disciple of Jesus Christ; for now I begin really to follow my Saviour and my Master. My desires are accomplished. I have nothing now to ask my Lord, save that I may shed my blood for Him." It seems wonderful how such a course of life could be maintained amidst the sufferings of a Japanese prison, but the secret is discovered by those words of S. Theresa: "God helps those who, for His sake, undertake great things, and He never fails those who put their trust in Him alone."

The highest aspirations of Father Dominic's soul was fulfilled on September 8, 1628, the feast of the Nativity of Mary. On that day he was burnt alive, with Father Anthony of S Bonaventure, a Franciscan, Brother Thomas and Brother Anthony, professed Dominican lay-brothers, and

Brother Dominic, a Franciscan lay-brother.
Within the space of a few days his other companions, nearly all Tertiaries of S. Dominic, were
either burnt or beheaded.

Whilst being conducted to martyrdom, Father
Dominic saw Correia, a Portuguese, an intimate
friend of his, gazing at him with tears of sorrow
and compassion. "Nay, my friend," said the
holy Friar, "do not grieve, we are going to
heaven, and you must pray for us till the end."
He then took a handkerchief, dipped in the blood
of a martyr, and placing it reverently on his head,
he exclaimed: "Behold this is the ladder by
which we shall ascend to heaven." These
martyrs are among the beatified.

———

CHAPTER XII.

*Missionaries sent from Manilla. Martyrdom of
the last Dominicans in Japan.*

THE General Chapter of the Friars Preachers
assembled at Toulouse during the year
1628 took into consideration the afflicted state of
the Japanese Church, and ordained that the
largest possible number of missionaries should be
sent to its assistance. Directly the intelligence
of this order reached the Priory of Manilla, all
the fathers were anxious to depart immediately.

But obedience obliged many to remain, while certain favoured ones were chosen. Father Thomas of S. Hyacinth started forthwith, and arrived safely in Japan the year following. Father John of the Angels, was not so successful, being beheaded on his way by the inhabitants of the island of Loo-Choo. He had spent twenty-four years in Japan on a former occasion, having arrived there in 1607, and was therefore well versed in its difficult language, into which he had translated several religious works. His extreme devotion to the Holy Rosary, and the unction and energy with which he recommended it in his sermons, won for him the name, among the Japanese, of the Father of the Rosary. Many details of the marvellous graces given by means of the Rosary are mentioned by Advarte in his account of this father's labours. One old man, in a village of the kingdom of Arima, who had not been to confession for thirty years, and whom many missionaries had tried to convert, was brought to his duties almost immediately after Father John had enrolled him in the confraternity.

In the year following (1630) Father Hyacinth Esquivel, accompanied by a Franciscan missionary, endeavoured to reach Japan, but the precautions taken at every port made it almost as difficult to effect a landing as to escape detection when actually labouring in the empire. These two fathers were seized just before disembarking at Nagasaki, and were both beheaded.

Meanwhile the fury of the persecution was unabated, and in 1628 three more members of the Third Order of S. Dominic were beheaded for the faith at Nagasaki. Particular mention is made of these, because the circumstances of their martyrdom were carefully examined by the testimony of eyewitnesses, and they are amongst those beatified by Pius the Ninth. Their names were Michael, Paul, and Dominic, and they were selected for death on account of their generous zeal in assisting the Fathers of S. Dominic. Three hundred martyrs are known to have suffered between the beginning of 1629 and the end of 1632, but these are doubtless only few compared to the multitude whose names are forgotten on earth.

Father Dominic Erquicia, who had entered Japan after a long voyage of extreme difficulty and danger, with Father Lewis Bertrand in 1623, was, for the nine years he spent on the mission, in high repute for virtue and learning among heathens as well as Christians. The fruit of his self-denying labours was abundant in various parts of the Empire, and after suffering much in prison he was martyred with prolonged and terrible torture in the year 1633. A native brother who acted as his catechist, and had adopted the name of Francis, was the companion of his sufferings and his crown.

This martyrdom was soon followed by that of Father James of S. Mary, a native priest. He was the son of Christian parents in the kingdom of Omura, and received his education in the Jesuit college. For some time he preached among his countrymen, and gained many children for the Church, being a favourite of the higher classes, and even of the government officials, on account of his mental abilities and high culture. Finding, however, that his power for good was diminished by his being only a layman, he went to Manilla, with the intention of becoming a religious. He desired to enter the Order of S. Augustine, but difficulties arising, he dwelt for some time as a hermit on a mountain near the city. Hearing that native subjects were wanted by the Friars Preachers, he applied to Father Melchior Mencano, the Prior of Manilla, and was clothed in S. Dominic's habit on the feast of the Assumption, 1624. In the noviciate he displayed many religious virtues in a high degree, particularly extreme meekness under reproof, and therefore made his profession in due time, and received Holy Orders on August 15, 1626. After his arrival in his native country he remained hidden for some time in Nagasaki, administering the Sacraments among the afflicted Christians, and in 1633 received the crown of martyrdom, after acute sufferings, endured with invincible courage. His catechist, Michael, shared his glory.

Father Luke of the Holy Ghost, the companion of Father Lewis Bertrand, had escaped detection for nearly ten years, although the search made for missionaries never relaxed in vigilance. At one time he took refuge in the mountains, when for forty days he managed to maintain himself on some species of wild plant, while at another he travelled over great regions of country, evangelizing the people. Advarte gives a catalogue of the places he visited. He even penetrated into Makao, and was captured at last in company with a Jesuit Father named Anthony de Sousa. He was tortured in a most revolting way before his death, which, with two or three Brothers of the Third Order, he endured willingly for the love of Christ.

Unhappily space forbids more than a rapid mention of these different heroes of the faith, as illustrious during their lives as they were invincible amidst the torments of their last triumphs. Many interesting details are given about each in Advarte's long history of the Philippine Province. Father Jordan of S. Stephen, who arrived at Nagasaki during the year 1632, was a Sicilian, who had been attracted to the Eastern missions by the fame of the martyrs of Japan. After being clothed with the habit of S. Dominic in his native country, and studying in different Priories in Spain, he laboured for some time in the Philippine Islands amongst the Chinese, whose language he had completely mastered. He was a very learned theologian, and wrote several works of considerable merit, so that he is adorned in heaven with the three special aureolas of virgin, doctor and martyr. He arrived at Nagasaki in the disguise of a Chinaman after the evening had begun to close in, and having no guide, he was wandering about the streets trusting to God's providence, when he saw Father Dominic Erquicia standing at the door of a house. In spite of their disguise they recognized each other, and were soon locked in the tender embrace of brothers unexpectedly meeting in a strange land. Father Jordan assisted Father Dominic until his martyrdom, and then continued his labours, until his career as a missionary was cut short by his own capture, with Father Thomas of S. Hyacinth, during the course of the next year. Father Thomas was a Japanese, who had been professed and ordained in the Priory at Manilla, and had already laboured as a missionary in the island of Formosa, and for nine years in his own country. Marina of Omura, a member of the Third Order, was arrested with the two priests. Another Tertiary, Magdalen of Nagasaki, deserves special notice, as it appears that God inspired her to deliver herself up to martyrdom. Hearing of Father Jordan's imprisonment, she boldly presented herself before the guards, demanding admission in order to be professed in the Third Order, in which she was only a novice. The cruel

L

Japanese soldiers were touched with compassion and admiration at her courage, and tried to persuade her to retire, and not to force them to arrest her as a Christian. "I am a Christian," she exclaimed, "and, what is more, a Religious, the spiritual daughter of Father Jordan, and it is your duty to apprehend me." Her desire was gratified, and all these four martyrs expired by inches, after a series of torments, suggested by the ingenious cruelty of their persecutors.

After the numerous martyrdoms of 1633 the Church in Japan presented a deplorable aspect. Glorious as the persecution had doubtless been, and numberless as were the white-robed martyrs with which it had peopled Heaven, still these were times in which the fervent alone could be Christians. Many therefore, unable to resist the trial, denied their faith, and thus purchased safety. Finding themselves again orphans, bereaved prematurely of those fathers sent to their assistance, the poor Christians once more raised a cry of distress, which was answered by the Friars Preachers of Manilla. Four of their number determined, under the sanction of obedience, to brave every danger, and to venture into the forbidden regions of Japan. These were Fathers Anthony Gonzales, Michael Ozarata, William Courtet, and Vincent of the Cross.

Father Anthony Gonzales was a man of remarkable holiness of life, endowed with all the qualities that form the perfect religious, and particularly excelling in that which includes and implies all the rest, the gift of continual prayer. Devoted as he was to the active life of the apostolate, like a true Dominican, he never suffered its harassing cares to interrupt his union with God and constant familiar conversation with Him. A native of Spain, where he made his profession, he left his own country for Manilla out of love for souls. He was first employed as regent of studies, for he was remarkable no less as a theologian than as a holy religious.

Father Michael Ozarata was also a Spaniard, and was professed in the Priory of S. Thomas in Madrid, where for some years he remained in the peaceful happiness of a strict convent. At this time many seculars were leaving their homes, and bidding farewell to their friends, to make their fortunes in the colonies dependent on the Spanish crown. Father Michael, considering this, determined to undertake, for an incorruptible crown, what so many of his countrymen were doing for a perishable reward, and, bidding adieu to his brethren and the beloved seclusion of his convent, he started to Manilla, where he remained till despatched to Japan. Out of devotion to the Mother of God he had taken the name of Michael of the Rosary.

Father William Courtet was a Frenchman, and Advarte speaks in the highest terms of his eminent holiness. The French Province had just been reformed and restored to primitive fervour and regularity, when Father William, as a youth, became a member of the Toulouse Province, and made his profession on the feast of the Assumption in the year 1608. During his long course of theological study, he was a model of religious virtue, and was afterwards Master of Novices and Professor of Theology in the Priory of Toulouse. A difficult and delicate office was then assigned him. A religious was wanted in the ancient Priory of Avignon, to restore strict discipline within its walls. Father Courtet combined all those rare qualities necessary for a successful reformer, and was sent to Avignon as Prior and Lector. The fervour of the new Prior, tempered with prudent charity, soon established and confirmed that strict observance of which he gave a model in his own practice. But while thus serving the Order at Avignon, an old desire awoke within his breast. He had been first attracted to the Friars Preachers in his early years by hearing of the virtues and heroic courage of their martyred brethren in Japan. And now he sought and obtained permission from Nicholas Ridolphi, the Master General, to follow in their footsteps. To the regret of the French Province he therefore travelled to Madrid, walking all the way on foot, in great poverty, and taking every opportunity of benefiting souls during his journey. During the time he remained at Madrid, he was highly esteemed for his love of observance, and reaching the Philippine Islands, he was detained for some time at Manilla as professor of theology, where he effected much good by his learning, and the example of his holy life. Besides attending with the utmost regularity, during the two hours devoted in that Priory to meditation in community, he spent much extra time in prayer, and the frequency of his conversation with God was proved by the strictness with which he observed the silence prescribed by the rule. During the last years of his life he never used a bed, and his nights were chiefly spent in prayer. Whilst at Manilla he declined to take the usual precautions to protect himself against the mosquitos, which swarm there, offering to God the acute suffering they occasioned him as a mortification for his sins. Not content with this penance, he wore round his waist an iron girdle with fifteen circles of points so sharp as often to fetch blood, and this he bore in honour of the fifteen Mysteries of the Holy Rosary. His discipline was most severe, and every day he scourged himself in a spirit of deep repentance. So rigorous was the abstinence he habitually practised, that besides the ordinary fasts of the Order his food for three days in the week was simple bread and water. His love of silence and prayer, united with the modesty of his demeanour, won the esteem of his brethren,

who looked upon him as a saint.   As an instance
of his humility it is related that one day, in a
theological disputation in the students' classes,
some unguarded words escaped him in the heat
of the discussion, and at the end of the class he
prostrated himself before his brother-lector, begging
pardon for what he had said.   Severely as he
treated himself, his gentleness and sympathy for
sinners was equally remarkable.   Every one who
sought his aid, departed consoled.

Father Vincent of the Cross was a Japanese,
born of Christian parents, who offered him to
God before his birth.   He received his education
in the Jesuit college in Nagasaki, and when
the persecution broke up the college, he went
to Manilla, where he dwelt for some time, and
returning to preach to his countrymen, was
ordained priest, and afterwards admitted into the
Order of S. Dominic, about a year before his
martyrdom.

These missionaries, accompanied by two seculars, reached the island of Loo-Choo in July,
1636, and not being able to proceed, they
laboured for some time in that and neighbouring
islands. . It appears that they were never able
to penetrate into the Empire itself, but were
recognised and conducted to Nagasaki, bound
as captives, on September 13, 1637.   Before the
tribunal of the judge they boldly confessed that
they were priests, and religious of the Order of

S. Dominic, and that, although they were well aware of the emperor's edicts, they had entered Japan in order to preach the true faith and console the afflicted Christians. Finding they could not be shaken by threats, the judges determined to employ torture, and in this they discovered a truly diabolical ingenuity. Several different times an almost incredible amount of water was poured down their throats, and then forced through the mouth and nose by means of extreme pressure. Father Anthony Gonzales hardly survived the infliction of this torment, and being carried back to prison, he shortly after bid a tender farewell to his companions, and gave up his soul to God on September 24, 1637. The heathens vented their malice on his senseless corpse, which they burnt, afterwards casting the ashes into the sea.

Father Vincent of the Cross was for a moment overcome by the intensity of his sufferings, and consented to abjure his faith. No sooner, however, had the shameful words of apostasy crossed his lips than he felt a bitter remorse, and yielding to the earnest exhortations of his companions, he again boldly confessed the sacred Name of Jesus Christ.

They were next tortured with long sharp awls that were thrust under the nails even to the first joint of the fingers, but this excruciating agony wrung from them no words unworthy of a

Christian; they only exclaimed, "How sweet it is to suffer! Queen of the Holy Rosary, pray for us." The executioners in astonishment rattled the handles of the awls together, and the martyrs replied, "How sweet a music is this for heaven!" When the blood dropped upon the ground, one of the martyrs in a transport of love cried out: "Behold those beautiful roses! I have dyed them, sweet Jesus, for Thy love in my blood; but what are these few drops compared to the torrent of blood Thou didst shed for my sake?" They were then obliged to scratch the ground with the protruding handles of the awls, but no torment could shake their constancy.

At this dreadful spectacle the bystanders wept with compassion, and the executioners themselves, moved by such an exhibition of heroic generosity, complained of the folly that could induce men so noble-hearted and courageous to come into Japan merely to undergo a death of protracted suffering. "We came not hither," replied Father Courtet, "for the sole object of being tortured to death; but we came to preach the true religion, and to convince men of the folly of idol worship."

After the torture had lasted a considerable time, nature became completely exhausted, and the martyrs fell back with their eyes closed, apparently almost lifeless. This was seized upon as a successful moment to tempt them to apostatise, but the question was no sooner put than

life and vigour seemed to return, for the martyrs
cried out aloud: "We are deaf to all such
proposals; we have not come to Japan to be
guilty of such weakness." Seeing that nothing
could shake their constancy, the soldiers carried
them back to prison on litters.

A day or two later, the moment of their last
triumph arrived. After being paraded round the
streets of Nagasaki, the martyrs were conducted
to that famous hill on which so many Christian
warriors had already won the crown of victory.
Here five pits had been prepared, and over each
a martyr was suspended with his head downwards. Their feet were tightly bound to a
horizontal beam, and half their bodies were in
the pit, which was then covered with boards
so arranged that they pressed the victim down,
and so increased the intensity of his suffering.
This agony, declared by the executioners to be
intolerable, continued for two days and nights,
but God supported His servants, and their
courage was not exhausted. The only sounds
heard issuing from those pits of torture were
earnest prayers, or the voice of one sufferer
exhorting his companions to perseverance. On
the morning of the third day, the pits being
uncovered, the two seculars were found dead,
but in the three religious some sparks of life
still faintly lingered. The command was to
behead those who might be discovered alive,

and this sentence was carried out on Father Vincent of the Cross, as he lay prostrate, totally unable to kneel. Father Michael Ozarata and Father William Courtet had sufficient strength to embrace each other tenderly. "We have much to talk over," said they, "but we will leave all till we meet in heaven." Side by side then knelt these two brothers; the executioner's sword descended as the Names of Jesus and Mary were on their lips. These are called by Father Alexander de Rhodes, of the Society of Jesus, "the greatest martyrs of Japan," and it is indeed astonishing to reflect on the length and intensity of their sufferings and the cheerful fortitude they displayed.

Although these martyrs are not included in the list of the beatified, which extends only to the year 1632, whereas they suffered on September 27, 1636, it is a fitting termination to the long series of heroic conflicts by which the Friars Preachers distinguished themselves in Japan. It is the last Dominican martyrdom of which any account remains, though no doubt many Tertiaries and Rosarians continued to be chosen as victims for the sacrifice as long as the persecution lasted.

CHAPTER XIII.

Missionaries unable to enter Japan. The Dutch.
The late Discovery of Christians. Conclusion.

FTER the martyrdom recorded in the last
chapter, the Japanese Church was in a
most deplorable state of destitution. It became,
however, impossible for the most devoted missionaries to supply the place of their martyred
brethren, for a law was made by which at every
landing-place of the empire, the sacred symbol
of the Cross was placed, and officers were appointed with the strictest orders to oblige every
foreigner who might attempt to disembark, to
trample upon the Cross in sign of hatred of the
Christian faith. Any one refusing was arrested,
or at least forbidden to land. Besides this,
another edict obliged every subject of the
emperor to wear publicly an idol, or some other
evident sign of heathenism, by which all the
members of the prescribed religion might be immediately recognised. These measures, stringently
carried out, deprived Christians of all hope of
obtaining a fresh supply of priests. They were
left without sacraments or Sacrifice, to the mercy
of their bitter enemies. Active persecution for

some time continued.   The climax of all was reached in the year 1638, and the sun of Christianity appeared then indeed to sink for ever, and dark night to become universal over the whole land.   Owing to the tyranny and exactions of the governors of the province of Arima, the population rose in rebellion, and with hope of alleviating their hard lot the Christians, numbering still, in spite of the bitter persecution, many thousands, joined the rebel forces.   They took refuge in a strongly fortified place called Phimabara which was besieged by the imperial army, and though a gallant resistance was made for 102 days, the garrison was at last over-powered and an indiscriminate slaughter ensued. In this siege the Dutch rendered considerable assistance to the imperial army by lending artillery and ammunition.   The number of those massacred is given by the Dutch general as amounting to 40,000, and among them all the Christian auxiliaries.

After the failure of this Japanese " Pilgrimage of Grace " little is known of the history of the Christian population.   In 1640 the Portuguese despatched an embassy to the emperor with the hope of making such arrangements as would enable them once more to enter the empire for trade, but the ambassadors were murdered at Nagasaki, and their remains, enclosed in a chest, were sent back to Macao, with the following inscription : " As long as the sun continues to shine on the earth, let no Christian dare to enter Japan, and let every one understand that if the king of Spain himself, or the God of the Christians, or even the great Xaca (one of the principal deities of Japan), should violate this law, they shall be punished with death." This insolent inscription, truly diabolical in the intensity and folly of its blasphemy, was put up on notice boards all over the empire, at landing-places, ferries and in other public positions for the space of two hundred years as a constant protest against the proscribed religion.

To render it impossible for any Christian native to remain undetected, a new national festival was instituted under the title of " The Feast for Trampling on the Image." All the inhabitants, especially in regions where the Christian religion had chiefly flourished, were required to join in this abominable ceremony, which consisted in trampling on the Cross and a likeness of our Lady and her Divine Son. At Nagasaki the festival lasted for four whole days after the beginning of each new year, which commences in Japan on February 19.

After the murder of the Portuguese ambassadors in 1640 none but Chinese [*] and Dutch ships were allowed to trade with Japan,

* In 1647 five Friars Preachers tried to effect a landing in Japan, but the attempt was unsuccessful.

and these were only permitted to enter the port of Nagasaki. The Dutch were no more considered to be Christians than the Chinese. The Japanese argued very sensibly that a man who would trample on the Cross could not belong to the religion of the Crucified. The Dutch merchants were treated in the most ignominious manner, but they willingly endured insults of every kind in order to secure some commercial advantage. They were confined to one small island, connected with Nagasaki by a bridge, and the gates were carefully locked at night and guarded by native soldiers. No Dutchman was allowed to have a light in his house at night, and each ship was visited on its arrival by officers, who carried away the sails, guns, and rudders, which were retained until the departure of the ship. They were likewise strictly forbidden to hold any kind of religious service. Even as late as the year 1855, when some French vessels of war were lying in the harbour of Nagasaki, the chief man of the Dutch factory being invited by the officers to dinner, returned this answer : " I would willingly accept your invitation, but they will not allow me."

In the year 1709 a devoted Sicilian priest named Sidotti was determined to enter Japan, and accordingly landed upon the open coast. He baptized a few converts, but was captured almost immediately, and was shut up in a little hole, in which miserable den he lingered, preaching to such as visited him, till released by death.

There is one more matter of praiseworthy labour recorded of the ancient Catholic missionaries that is mentioned by Dr. Casartelli, which ought to be noted here. In the midst of their work and sufferings they found time to study the language and to write books of philology. "Protestant writers have recorded with astonishment the fact that whilst the Dutch, favoured as they were by the Japanese Government, did nothing in the cause of science, it is to the Catholic missionaries, in spite of the terrible times of persecution, that Europe owes the earliest works relating to the Japanese language and literature." Father J. Rodriguez, who reached Japan in 1583, published many important works from 1590 to 1610, and in 1595 the Jesuits in Amahusa printed a Portuguese-Latin dictionary. "The Dominicans rivalled the Jesuits in their literary zeal. Diego Collado was a Dominican, whose dictionary and grammar of the Japanese language appeared in Rome in 1632. Three years before, the Dominicans of Manilla had printed a Spanish translation of the Jesuit dictionary. . . . . A number of religious works in the Japanese language for the use of native Christians were compiled and published by the Christian missionaries. Bishop Serqueryza, a

Jesuit, composed a work on moral theology. One of the Franciscan fathers was a native Japanese, who besides translating the *Flos Sanctorum* into his mother tongue, published also a Japanese grammar and a Spanish-Latin-Japanese dictionary." *

From 1638 until the middle of this century there is nothing to record, but in 1831 a vessel was wrecked on the coast of the Philippine Islands, and the Japanese sailors who manned it were found wearing Christian emblems, declared themselves to have been baptized and to have been instructed in the Christian religion by the tradition of their ancestors. In 1846, the Sovereign Pontiff Gregory XVI. appointed M. Augustus Forçade, a member of the Society of Foreign Missions, first Vicar Apostolic of Japan and the isles of Loo-Choo ; but no entrance was effected into the empire till 1856, in which year there was a renewal of the persecution against the native Christians. Owing to the treaties between France and the Japanese Government, two priests of the Foreign Missions were able to build a church at Yokohama, a town near the city of Yeddo. Communication with the natives was strictly forbidden, the church being only tolerated for the use of Europeans. In the year 1863 the two missionaries, MM. Furet and

* See Dr. Casartelli's article in the *Dublin Review* for April, 1895.

Petitjean, collected funds for a church in Nagasaki, which was dedicated under the patronage of S. John the Baptist. This church was the scene of a wondrous event. On March 17, 1865, certain Japanese presented themselves to the missionaries, and announced that they were Christians, and that in the village to which they belonged, thirteen hundred still remained faithful to the true religion. The joy which filled the hearts of the missionaries at this intelligence was increased almost daily by the fresh discoveries they made of Christian congregations, numbering 2,500 in the country round Nagasaki, and thousands more in different parts of the Empire.*
These Christians, though none of them had ever seen a priest or heard a Mass, were found to be well instructed in the essential doctrines of religion, and were familiar with many of the prayers in common use among the faithful.

This fact must be acknowledged to be one of the strongest proofs on record of the divine vitality of the Catholic faith. The first introduction of Christianity into the Empire and its rapid spread among the people were sufficient of themselves to establish the identity of the religion that had such mysterious power over the heathen Empire of the extreme East in the

* Full particulars of this wonderful discovery will be found in the *Annals of the Propagation of the Faith* for March, 1868.

sixteenth century, with the religion that conquered the old Roman Empire in the first ages of Christianity. But the conquest of heathen empires, the civilization of barbarous nations, by the introduction of Christian faith and Christian morals is a common event in the history of the Church, and only a token of God's ordinary providence. What is so extraordinary a manifestation of God's power and of the fatherly care with which He watches over His Church, is the fact of these poor Japanese persevering in the true faith and remaining fervent Catholics, though for more than two hundred years they have lived without priests, without Sacraments and Sacrifice, without schools and books, and threatened with the most terrible penalties if they manifested their secret belief. This is a work as purely supernatural, as much beyond human power as the raising of the dead to life, and it reveals, in the clearest possible light, the Divine origin and life of the Catholic Church. All human agency is here removed, and we stand face to face with the direct work of God for His Church. A rapid glance over the Christian annals of Japan will enable the reader to estimate this fact more justly.

The first missions in Japan, begun by St. Francis Xavier, were crowned with the most brilliant success. In spite of prejudice, hatred of foreign influence, love of ease, strong adherence to ancient customs, and dearly-cherished superstitions, the Christian faith, though doing violence to all these, was no sooner proclaimed than it spread over the whole Empire, and took the deepest root in the hearts of the people. The country seemed ripe for conversion. Men of every class professed and practised Christianity, from the princes and governors on their thrones to the lepers that lay neglected on the roadside. Churches were opened, the public service of the Church was fully carried out, Mass was sung by Japanese ecclesiastics, and processions moved in state through the streets of Nagasaki. Colleges were founded to supply a native priesthood, hospitals arose for the sick and for the care of foundlings ; confraternities, as those of the Rosary and the Holy Name, registered thousands of native converts amongst their members. Religious Orders also found Japan a genial soil, and houses were springing up in all parts— convents of the Friars of S. Dominic, S. Francis, and S. Augustine, and colleges of the sons of S. Ignatius. Everything seemed to foretell that before long Japan would be a Catholic nation.

What interrupted this happy prospect? What instrument was employed by the evil spirit to stir up persecution against this Church, so young, yet of such fair promise? In Japan, as elsewhere, Protestantism was the arch-enemy of Christianity. But for the Reformation there seems every reason to suppose that Japan would now be a Catholic empire, and that native bishops of Nagasaki and Yeddo would have sat in the General Council of the Vatican. Partly through commercial jealousy of the Spaniards, partly through fanatical religious hatred, the Dutch Protestants excited the emperor against the missionaries. The same spirit that caused the Dutch to torture the martyrs of Gorcum, the French Huguenots to throw forty Jesuit missionaries into the sea on their voyage to Brazil, ...raise the persecu...ish to make it a capital crime to say and Japan is a heathen lan...ies, instigated the sectaries The persecution that their ...an. They succeeded, was not surpassed in atrocity by the of Nero or Diocletian; while the heroismnies excited martyrs rivalled that displayed by the Ch..secutions of the early Church. That this is no exaggera.of the recent authors both Catholic and Protestant ampians testify. "Since the apostolic times," says Louveion "no grander spectacle had been exhibited to the'v Christian world. It embraced episodes beautiful enough to delight the angels, and refinements of wickedness sufficient to excite the jealousy of demons." In fact, as far as can be ascertained, over one thousand members of the four religious bodies, the Jesuits, Franciscans, Dominicans and Augustinians, sealed their faith with their blood, and over 200,000 native Japanese put on the white robe of the martyrs.

In many points this persecution bears strong resemblance to that which raged in England after the Reformation.   In Japan as in England political necessity was pleaded as a justification of measures which had for their object the extinction of the Catholic faith.   From their insular position the Governments of both countries derived considerable assistance in their design, as it enabled them in great measure to enforce the law by which the entrance of missionaries was forbidden.

The heathen in the one country and the heretic in the other for many years employed fire and sword to extirpate the Christian faith.   For a time the powers of darkness seemed to hold undisputed sway, and in England and Japan it was the boast of the Government to have purged their realms of all popish taint.   But in neither country did the boast prove true.   Catholics have remained in each, in spite of the efforts of their foes.   But the difference between the two countries lay in this, that the Japanese, owing to their empire being remote and inaccessible to Europeans, were able more completely to exclude missionaries, and therefore we should have expected that very few Catholics would be found remaining.   There never was a period when the Church in England was entirely without pastors.   But for nearly two hundred years no priest said Mass in Japan.   In England the Catholic faith had been for centuries the established religion, the whole nation had belonged to its communion, its traditions were firmly rooted in the oldest institutions of the country. In Japan the faith had never been more than a foreign intrusion preached by strangers, and involving a complete revolution of thought and action in any native who embraced its teaching. Yet in Japan, large numbers by God's grace have preserved their faith intact, and these Christians who have had no priest among them for two centuries, are not only on their guard against idolatry, but are fully aware that there are spurious Christians, wolves in the clothing of sheep, who seek to disperse the flock. They know also the test of the true faith. The French missionaries tell us that one of the questions they ask is the following :

"'Your kingdom and that of Rome, are they of one mind ? '

"'Have you been sent by the great Chief of the kingdom of Rome?' On receiving answers in the affirmative they seemed greatly pleased."

What is this but expressing in their simple way the same rule of faith as that given by the learning of S. Ambrose, *Ubi Petrus, ibi Ecclesia ?*

The other points upon which they anxiously questioned the missionaries were as to their celibacy as priests, and the honour they paid to the Blessed Virgin. Having obtained satisfactory answers on these subjects, they joyfully recognized in M. Petitjean the successor of their ancient apostles.

The catechists or baptisers in the different Christian villages were examined by the missionaries, and it was ascertained that they had preserved the form of baptism with the utmost accuracy.*

What explanation can be offered for this wonderful fact? Without the direct assistance of God, and the pleading of the martyrs' blood, it would have been impossible. It bears the strongest testimony to the truth of the Catholic Church, which can thus sustain its life, drawn from a Divine source, under circumstances that must crush any religion of human origin. No religion ever professed on earth can present a fact so astounding and so significant. The veil must indeed be closely drawn over the eyes of those who do not recognize in this the finger of God. "By their fruits you shall know them," is the touchstone given to us to discover the teachers of truth; and in Japan the good seed scattered by the missionaries two centuries ago is still bearing ample fruit, in spite of the persevering efforts of the heathen to uproot it.

Traces of the different religious Orders which sent missionaries to Japan are still visible in the names of villages and of individual Christians. S. Francis Xavier and S. Clare are two of the Catholic settlements, and one of the most fervent catechists had received the name of Dominic.

* For further details, see the *Annals of the Propagation of the Faith* for March, 1868.

A picture of the fifteen mysteries of the Rosary was held in great veneration, as tradition points it out as the property of the early missionaries, and it has been instrumental in keeping alive the faith in the events of our Lord's life.

Pius IX. with joyful thanksgiving for so wonderful an event established a feast, under the title of " The Finding of the Christians," which is celebrated in all the Catholic churches of Japan every year on March 17, the day on which in 1865 the hidden Christians manifested themselves. In 1866 the same Pontiff appointed Father Petitjean the first Vicar Apostolic of Japan. During the next year 1867 the new bishop erected a statue in honour of "Our Lady of Japan," and in the same year Pius IX. beatified two hundred and five of the Japanese martyrs, both European and native, as will be seen from the list of the Dominican martyrs at the end of this volume.

Not yet however were the days of persecution for this much suffering and long enduring Church at an end. The cup of its sufferings had not been drained to the last bitter dregs. The newly discovered Christians were soon again under persecution for professing a religion still forbidden under pain of death, and they showed the same heroic spirit which had animated their martyred forefathers. The government, while allowing a church to be built in Yokohama, had shown its old hatred for the faith by stipulating that

it must be used exclusively for the benefit of
Europeans. When it was found that the Christian natives were in communication with the
missionaries and refused to recognize the bonzes,
an active persecution arose. In 1868 a fresh
edict was displayed on the public notice boards
which declared that "The evil sect called
Christian is strictly forbidden. Suspicious persons should be reported to the proper officers,
and rewards will be given." Hundreds of Christians were dragged before the judges, interrogated
as to their religion, and after boldly confessing
their faith were thrown into prison and sent
into exile. According to one account a body
of Christians amounting to three hundred were
condemned to death, and being taken out in a
ship, were thrown into the deep sea.

From this date 1868, the very year in which
Japan adopted in so wonderful a manner western
ideas and manners, until 1873 when all persecution ceased, though the severity of the persecution
could not be compared to the ancient one, still it
was by no means merely nominal. According to
trustworthy statistics many thousands of Christians
were persecuted by imprisonment and exile, and
many were so tortured that nearly two thousand
gave their lives for the love of Christ.

When the intelligence of this state of affairs
reached Europe, it roused deep sympathy for the
sufferers, and Pius IX. sent letters to encourage

these Christian confessors to be valiant and to walk fearlessly in the footprints of their heroic forefathers. The Powers also remonstrated with the Japanese government, but for some time with no success, the answer being that the missionaries were disturbers of the public peace, and the Mikado seemed, in spite of his adoption of Western civilization in the material order, to be determined to follow the example of his ancestors, and to wage war to the death against Christianity.

But a brighter day was near, and in 1873 the Mikado, who had introduced constitutional government into the empire and had abolished the Shogunate, began to tolerate Christianity and released all who had lost their liberty for their faith, and at once the persecuted Church began to revive. Though there were only three missionary priests in 1860, the number in 1891 had risen to eighty-two, and nuns of different Congregations had been introduced, and before long many natives joined their ranks and have been professed. "The first native nun, at least in modern times, and also the first to die, was Agatha Kataoka Fuku, in religion Sister Margaret, the the sister and daughter of martyrs, who herself died quite young from the effects of the ill-usage she had endured as a child in gaol, when she saw her father perish under the blows of the executioner." *

* Casartelli, *Dublin Review*, l.c.

In 1891, by an apostolic Letter of June 15, Pope Leo XIII. created a hierarchy consisting of one archbishop with three suffragan sees for the empire of Japan. The capital city of Tokio, the residence of the Emperor, is the see of the archbishop, while the Bishop of Hakodate has charge of all north of the archdiocese including the "curious aboriginal race, the Ainas, of Yezo, the evangelization of whom was seriously taken in hand by Bishop Berlioz in 1893." The Bishop of Nagasaki has spiritual charge of a large part of south Japan, containing more than 31,674 Catholics; and the diocese of Osaka comprises what was formerly the vicariate of Central Japan.

In the first edition of this little volume are the words, " Protestant missionaries are unheard of in Japan," but the writer ventured then to foretell that directly the empire was in a safe condition and persecution had ceased, " we shall no doubt be informed, as was the case when Dr. Smith went to China, that the first herald of the Gospel has started for Japan." Since the Buddhist religion has been disestablished and all persecution has ceased, Japan has been invaded by Protestant missionaries of every sect. But times have changed, and feeling towards the Catholic Church has changed with them, for instead of ignoring or abusing the Catholic missions, Mr. Cobbold, the author of a short but interesting work called *Religion in Japan*, speaks in high terms of the work past and present of the Catholic missionaries.

"Turning now," he writes, " to the condition of Christian missions at the present day, it seems right to commence with those of the (Roman) * Catholic Church. Not only has the (Roman) Catholic Church in Japan a history which extends over three hundred years, but it reckons at the present time considerably more than double the number of adherents claimed by any other Christian body. Its influence has been particularly successful in the Goto Islands, in the neighbourhood of Nagasaki, where the devoted labours of the missionaries have won over a considerable portion of the population." † In the appendix will be found some statistics of the Catholic missions at the present time.

Mr. Cobbold proceeds to speak of the work of the Catholic missionaries by saying that " it is commended on all sides ; a prominent feature in their methods being a consideration for and adaptation to the habits and prejudices of the people that greatly facilitate their progress, especially among the poor of the country districts."

* I put " Roman " in brackets because, though we glory in our union with the See of Rome, to call ourselves Roman Catholics implies what we cannot admit, that a man may be a Catholic without being in communion with the See of Rome.

† Cobbold, *Religion in Japan*.

The whole number of Catholics amounts at present to something over 45,000.

There are now missionaries of the Russian schismatic Church, who have erected a Cathedral in Tokio and number about 20,000; of the Protestant Church of England presided over by by an Anglican Bishop; of the Protestant church of America, and of most of the Protestant nonconformist sects, among them "American and Canadian Methodists, Baptists, Swiss Protestants, American Friends, Scandinavian Church and Unitarians, raising the sum total of Protestant sects of all denominations to about 34,000 according to their own statistics."

These gentlemen of the various missionary societies are no doubt animated with the best intentions. It is a curious fact, however, to notice how courageously they have flocked to Japan now that all persecution has ceased and everything is perfectly safe. None of them can boast of a single martyr. And what is the inevitable effect of their presence and their hopeless differences of "religious opinion" on the clever Japanese? Evidently it must make Christianity ridiculous and suggest the very simple retort:—Before coming so many thousand miles to teach us, you had better agree among yourselves as to what Christianity is and what you believe yourselves.

That this strikes intelligent Protestants

themselves can be easily proved by one or two
extracts from recent works on Japan.

Miss Bickersteth, the sister of the late Protestant missionary Bishop in the empire, writes on
this subject as follows : " It was impossible not
to be struck with the present complication of
religious matters in the country as compared
with the days of Xavier. Then, on the one side,
there was the Buddhist-Shinto creed, undermined
by no Western science, still powerful in its
attraction for the popular mind, and presenting
a more or less solid resistance to the foreign
missionary ; and on the other hand, Christianity,*
as represented by Roman Catholicism, imperfect
truly, but without a rival in dogma or ritual.
Now the ranks of Buddhist-Shintoism are hope-
lessly broken ; the superstition of its votaries is
exposed by the strong light of modern science,
and their enthusiasm too often quenched in the
deeper darkness of Atheism.   Christianity, though
present in much greater force than in the days of
Xavier, is, alas, not proportionally stronger.   The
divisions of Christendom are nowhere more evident than in its foreign missions to an intellectual
people like the Japanese.   The Greek, the Roman,
the Anglican churches, the endless splits of Non-

* Is it more or less "imperfect" to preach one consis-
tent doctrine and to die for it, as the Catholic missionaries
did, than to have Christianity torn to pieces by a dozen
contending sects, without mission and without authority ?

conformity must present to the Japanese mind a bewildering selection of possibilities in religious truth."*

Bewildering indeed and likely to make Christianity a mockery to the heathen. " At the best," chimes in Mr. Cobbold, "so long as Romanists, Orthodox, Anglicans and Sectarians adhere to the positions they at present occupy, so long must any real unity of action be impossible ; neither can peace be sought by surrender or compromise of principle. But, meanwhile, there is of course a lamentable want of compactness among the converts. As a recent writer in the *Japanese Mail* remarked, ' they are more like scattered groups of soldiers than an army,' while the perplexity occasioned to those we are seeking to convince is terrible and great." †

This then is one of the most formidable obstacles to the conversion of Japan, producing a "terribly great perplexity in the heathen mind, owing to the hopeless divisions among the teachers." Protestantism and the Protestant principle of private judgment is the cause of those divisions ; therefore Protestantism is, by the confession of its own friends, the greatest and most terrible obstacle to the spread of Christianity. In the sixteenth and seventeenth centuries the Protestants helped

---

* *Japan as We saw It.* By Miss Bickersteth. Sampson Low, 1893.

† Cobbold, *Religion in Japan.*

the persecutors; in the nineteenth they form the most formidable obstacle to the work of the Catholic Church by making Christianity a byword for hopeless dissension and discord.

Another lamentable check to the conversion of Japan is the present indifference of the people to all religion. They are engrossed in the idea of material prosperity. The Buddhist religion has lost or is losing its hold upon their minds, and they desire to substitute no other in its place. Mgr. Cousin, the present Bishop of Nagasaki, complains in sad tones of "the evergrowing indifference of the population in regard to religious matters. This indifference is produced by books, newspapers, the official education, and the thirst for material well-being for which the extension of of commerce and relations with the outer world have opened up new resources." *

Mr. Cobbold also complains of the same indifference, for in his *Religion in Japan* we learn on page 109 that "a dull apathy as regards religion has settled down on the educated classes of Japan. The gods of heathenism have crumbled to nothing before modern science and civilization, and the glimmer of light and truth to which they pointed has gone as well."

But the blood of such a noble army of martyrs that has been shed in Japan cannot have been

* Compte-Rendu, page 48, quoted in the *Dublin Review.*

poured out in vain. In spite of indifference, in spite of Protestantism and all other obstacles, surely the truth will in the end prevail. For this must we pray. English Catholics especially should pray for the foreign missions, and make every sacrifice to help them, even if they can contribute only a mite to the good work. We are members of an immense colonial empire, on which the sun never sets. If our nation had retained the faith, that colossal empire would have been Catholic. But the history of foreign missions since the Reformation proves only too clearly that Protestantism has been one of the most fatal obstacles to the conversion of heathen nations. We shall therefore bring down the blessing of God on England by striving our utmost by fervent prayer and liberal alms to undo this work of evil, and to spread the faith in Japan and the other infidel nations.

It is earnestly to be hoped that before long the various Religious Orders that two hundred years ago furnished so many zealous apostles and heroic martyrs to the Japanese Church, may again be represented in the Empire, and that houses of Jesuits and Augustinians, Franciscans and Dominicans, may once more appear at Nagasaki and Tokio. The loud cry arising from the blood of so many martyrs now raised to the altars of the Church cannot remain unheard. With God's blessing the Confraternity of the Rosary will again number thousands of Japanese among its members, and Friars of S. Dominic will preach to the people, reminding them of the days they have heard of from their fathers, when Alphonsus Navarette and his companions carried the light of the true faith into Japan, and witnessed to its truth with their blood.

APPENDIX

IF any of our readers desire a full and authentic account of the history of the Catholic Church in Japan, especially in recent times, they will find it in a book lately published in France. Its title is, *La Religion de Jésus ressuscitée au Japon dans la seconde moitié du XIXe siècle*, par Francisque Marnas, missionaire apostolique, Vicaire Général Honoraire du Diocèse d'Osaka. (Paris: Delhomme et Briguet.) At the end of the second volume some interesting statistics will be found giving the state of the infant Church in 1895, and the progress made since 1860. In those thirty-five years, in spite of every difficulty and with very slender means, much has, thank God, been accomplished.

In 1860 all that can be recorded is that there were in Japan a prefect apostolic and two missionaries. The first vicar apostolic from 1866 to 1884 was Bishop Petitjean, to whom the hidden Christians made themselves known in 1865. This wonderful event is described in full detail by M.

Marnas. In 1880 there were two vicars apostolic and one auxiliary bishop, assisted by forty missionaries, twenty-seven nuns and thirty-eight catechists. The number of churches and chapels was eighty, and of schools and orphanages sixty-seven with 3,139 pupils, the number of the faithful being 23,909.

The hierarchy was established in 1891. In 1895 there were an archbishop and three bishops. These prelates were then assisted by eighty-eight European missionaries, and twenty Japanese priests, and 304 catechists. The number of churches and chapels had risen to 169, the schools and orphanages to 70, containing 5,479 pupils, while the Catholic population amounted to 50,302. Besides this there was a seminary for the training of native priests with forty-six students. A leper hospital had been established in Tokio containing seventy patients, and three other hospitals besides fifty-nine other medical centres. There were also twenty-five religious called in French " Marianites."

M. Marnas informs us (vol. II., p. 567) that the Trappist monks are going to form three establishments in Japan, and by this time they have probably begun their work. This is a special source of joy to any who have read of the magnificent work these monks have achieved in Africa. May their labours in Japan be crowned with a like success.

In 1895 the numbers in the Protestant missions amounted by their own statistics to 39,419, but these were divided into thirty-four different sects!

M. Marnas asks on page 567 (vol. II.) the momentous question, of such interest to all who love God, " What future has the Catholic Church before her in this country, where such extraordinary changes have taken place in so short a time? Evidently we can only form conjectures. But if we consider what has happened in Japan during the last thirty years, in a religious point of view only, we are surely justified in hoping for a magnificent development for the true faith."

A French lady, who will not allow her name to be published, has built a fine church at Nagasaki on the site of the great martyrdom.

LIST OF DOMINICAN MARTYRS IN JAPAN

I.—THOSE BEATIFIED BY PIUS THE NINTH.

PRIESTS.

1. Blessed Alphonsus Navarette, June 1, 1617. } *Spaniards.*
2. Blessed John of S. Dominic, 1619.
3. Blessed Lewis Florés, *Belgian*, 1622.
4. Blessed Francis Morales, *Spaniard*, 1622.
5. Blessed Angelo Orsucci, *Italian*, 1622.
6. Blessed Alphonsus de Mena, 1622.
7. Blessed Joseph of S. Hyacinth, 1622.
8. Blessed Hyacinth Orphanel, 1662.
9. Blessed Thomas of the Holy Ghost, 1622. } *Spaniards.*
10. Blessed Peter Vasquez, 1624.
11. Blessed Lewis Bertrand, 1627.
12. Blessed Dominic Castellet, 1628.

CHOIR-BROTHERS.

1. Blessed Alexis.
2. Blessed Thomas of the Rosary.
3. Blessed Dominic of the Rosary. } *Japanese.*
4. Blessed Mance of S. Thomas.
5. Blessed Dominic.

LAY-BROTHERS.

1. Blessed Mance of the Cross.
2. Blessed Peter of S. Mary.
3. Blessed Thomas of S. Hyacinth. } *Japanese.*
4. Blessed Anthony of S. Dominic.

THIRD ORDER.

1. Blessed Michael Diaz.
2. Blessed Paul Nangasci.
3. Blessed Thecla.
4. Blessed Peter.
5. Blessed Mary Tocuan.
6. Blessed Agnes Taquea.
7. Blessed Mary Xoum.
8. Blessed Gaspar Cotenda.
9. Blessed Francis.
10. Blessed Peter.
11. Blessed Lewis Giaciqui or Yakiki.
12. Blessed Lucy, his wife.
13. Blessed Andrew ⎫
14. Blessed Francis ⎬ his children.
15. Blessed Francis Curobiori.
16. Blessed Caius Jemon.
17. Blessed Magdalen Chiota.
18. Blessed Frances.
19. Blessed John Tomachi.
20. Blessed Dominic.
21. Blessed Michael.
22. Blessed Thomas.
23. Blessed Paul.
24. Blessed Romanus.
25. Blessed Leo.
26. Blessed James Fainscida.
27. Blessed Matthew Alvarez.
28. Blessed John Imamura.
29. Blessed Paul.
30. Blessed Michael Jamada.
31. Blessed Laurence.
32. Blessed Lewis Nisaci.
33. Blessed Francis.
34. Blessed Dominic.

II.—MARTYRS NOT BEATIFIED.

PRIESTS.

1. Father John of the Angels, 1629. ⎫
2. Father Hyacinth Esquivel, 1630. ⎬ *Spaniards.*
3. Father Dominic de Erquicia, 1633. ⎭
4. Father James of S. Mary, *Japanese*, 1633.
5. Father Luke of the Holy Ghost, *Spaniard*, 1633.
6. Father Thomas of S. Hyacinth, *Japanese*, 1633.
7. Father Jordan of S. Stephan, *Spaniard*, 1633.
8. Four Fathers mentioned by Father Charlevoix, names unknown, 1633.
9. Father Anthony Gonzales, 1637. ⎫
10. Father Michael Ozarata, 1637. ⎬ *Spaniards.*
11. Father William Courtet, *Frenchman*, 1637
12. Father Vincent of the Cross, *Japanese*, 1637.
13. Brother Francis, a *Japanese* lay-brother.

It would be impossible to collect and too long to give the names of the countless hosts of Tertiaries and Rosarians who are known, by human testimony, to have laid down their lives for Christ.   They will appear in the white-robed army on the great day of their triumph.

TE MARTYRUM CANDIDÁTUS LAUDAT EXERCITUS.

FINIS

ART AND BOOK COMPANY, PRINTERS, LONDON AND LEAMINGTON.

www.ingramcontent.com/pod-product-compliance
Lightning Source LLC
Chambersburg PA
CBHW030604040726
47497CB00008B/2840